The Game of Dostoevsky

THE
GAME
OF
DOSTOEVSKY

Samuel Astrachan

FARRAR,
STRAUS
AND
GIROUX
NEW
YORK

To Claude

CONTENTS

PART ONE
MONOPOLY

1

While an undergraduate at the University of Y in New York City, Edgar Hope, now an Instructor in English at the same university, made two friends with whom he thought he would always be in touch. His attachment to Max Wise and Luther Halverson had been deep, promoted by what his friends had offered him in the way of new ideas, by the experiences they had shared, and by his expectations for their futures. He had thought that given ten years, each would be as full of idealism as during college days and each would be successful in his field—Max would be the great American novelist; Luther would be a modern-day Clarence Darrow; and he, Edgar, would be a rising young professor, an authority on A, B, and C, who would write introductions to forgotten or ignored books which were required reading for every educated man, and who would, he had also fancied, now and then write some very good poetry.

With all his heart, Edgar had looked forward to periodic meetings with his friends, but circumstance being what it is, he had, once the second year after their graduation had passed, never met with either of them, and after the third year, never corresponded. Now, ten years had passed and when, one day early in September, 196–, Edgar happened to be glancing through a bulletin of his university and read that Max Wise had been appointed Assistant Professor of Russian Literature at the university, he felt little pleasure and some embarrassment at the possibility of a meeting.

Edgar Hope was a big, fair, good-looking fellow.

He was from Pontiac, Michigan, a small city with a small elite to which his family, his father being a physician with property holdings and business interests, belonged. When he was thirteen, he was sent to an Eastern boarding school where, during the next four years, he studied among other things Latin and Greek, played tennis, and nurtured already declared loves of literature and composition. He chose to attend the University of Y because it excelled in English studies and also because it was located near the center of New York City. He thought of theater, music, art galleries. And he was not disappointed. From the very first, he fell in love with his city. Friends, success in school work, and entry into various social circles came to him easily.

Upon being graduated, he was awarded a fellowship and went with it to England to study for a year. He re-read certain of Shakespeare's plays in order to date them, thus studying library and micro-film techniques, calligraphy, and the history of the time as scrounged up in a thousand

and one documents—letters about heavy rains, the sale of pigs, whooping coughs, marriages and deaths. He found his work an elegant waste of time and he persevered and did well. Upon his return to New York, he was offered and, after consulting his parents (through whom he would always be assured a comfortable income regardless of what he earned), accepted a position as Instructor of English at the University of Y.

Now, instructors are instructors and professors are professors. And though it is true that assistant professor is just one rank above instructor, the upper rank can be reached only by successful completion of the doctoral thesis. That Edgar, the favorite of many of his college professors, should have encountered difficulties in completing his thesis is not astonishing. Having passed all the written and oral examinations necessary with the thesis for the doctorate, he, who would have written a general appreciation of one of his favorite authors, found himself channeled by his doctoral committee into writing an evaluation of the theories of aesthetics embodied in the work of that author. And though many young men might make much of such a subject, no one, Edgar determined after a certain time, could make it interesting. Edgar, by now a devotee of vintage films, of atonal music as well as Mozart, of action painting as well as Piero della Francesca, a teacher with a class load of twelve hours a week, eighty or so papers to correct each week, found himself, to use his expression, 'hung up like Rod Steiger on an icehook in *On the Waterfront*.' He began his thesis every Christmas and summer vacation, but never kept with it for more than several days or thirty pages. He would start and the well-learned methods of exposition would keep him going a morning, an afternoon, but then he would look out the window for a minute too long, stare forlornly at the rooftops and sky and think of what his many acquaintances were doing; suddenly guilty, he would push aside his thesis and turn to a poem he had written six months before which he would now polish for the twentieth time. Sometimes, as if it were a proof of his integrity, he was proud of his inability to finish his thesis.

He was for a time indeed "hung up." He got high now and then on marijuana; for his poetry, he tried pharmaceutical kicks. He was able to recapture his former hopes only in the tone of his voice when, with youthful fervor, he read the poetry of the masters to his students. He turned cynic. He took to going on movie binges; he took to drinking a great deal of beer in a bar frequented by students. He developed a little paunch and a host of mannerisms to cover it up, verbal tics as well, holding forth before a group of students in bar or class and belligerently challenging after each of his statements, "Now is that not so?"

Then, barely one year before our story begins, he met a twenty-five-year-old woman through whose influence he found himself, or, at least someone who bore him a certain resemblance. He considered that he had an "understanding" with Miss Victoria Harm; he wrote more than a hundred pages of his thesis, every one of which he was sometimes proud of, showing off his erudition and intelligence, sentences of impeccable shape. With Miss Harm and a group of his and her friends, he had monthly teas which became bi-monthly meetings of a society—the Wolgamuts—and which, along with more private meetings with Miss Harm, his teaching and his steady work on his thesis, kept him very well occupied.

He spoke to Miss Harm about his former friend, Max Wise.

She had come to his apartment unexpectedly, as she sometimes did, just to spend a few minutes. They sat down in his study. He was in shirt sleeves, his collar open, smiling warmly, condescendingly, telling her how glad he was she had dropped by, clearly pleased that she had found him in the midst of his work, sentences still being formed in his head. He offered to make tea; passing his desk, he stopped to stack manuscript and carbon copies, to note down the opening phrase of a very nice sentence. The room was cozy and clean; books were piled carelessly in low cases; here and there on the walls were hung drawings Edgar had purchased from young artists who made the university area their stamping ground; one section of a wall was hung with *objets* he had picked up in his travels—miniatures in baroque frames, fine cracked porcelain—arranged in a clutter and, like the books, very neat. Late afternoon light dropped in through the window onto Edgar as he again took his seat, making his face all rose and clear, the walls rose, and only Victoria, deep in a big leather wingback chair, entirely in shadows.

"Lemon?"

"Thank you."

"Sugar?"

"No thank you."

Edgar sipped his tea. He smiled as if with the taste of lemon and said, "I have sketched in—have I not?—a bit of my career as a student. Well, I have just read that my old friend, Max Wise, I'm sure I have mentioned him before, will be teaching Russian Literature here at Y, as an assistant professor. It's ten years since I have last seen him, but of course I owe it to him to introduce him about. That is . . ."—with a wry smile—". . . if he wishes it. For it's true— is it not?—that a man might prefer a cell to the world (above all, a Russian scholar) or, might perversely prefer to force the lock on the door of the world rather than follow a friend who has the key. I am, my dear, speaking of course of you and our mutual friends, suggesting that I bring Max Wise, once I meet him, and if he is desirous of it, to one of our evenings."

Edgar hesitated but an instant. Victoria might be smiling, but he could not see. He continued: "Ten years, but I would be cheating were I to say that this is the first I have heard of dear Max. I have read his articles on Dostoevsky in various of our learned reviews. 'The Uses of Church Slavonic in *The Brothers Karamazov*' is one of his more recent titles and perhaps adequately describes the kind of work he is engaged in, admitting of course that he, like his soon-to-be *confrère*, might have begun his inquiry with the aim of writing 'Dostoevsky and Me,' or, 'Dostoevsky and God,' which title, it occurs to me, I may well offer to Max with the slight emendation: 'Dostoevsky and Deism,' the D's offering a nice drama and the word deism so much more appropriate to a scholarly tone than the word god."

Smiling at his invention, then sucking on his pipe, growing expansive as if he had sufficiently shown what had become of his friend, he said, "Max was to be the novelist. He had Zola-like ideas—stories about prostitutes and that sort of thing. He sympathized with the downtrodden; he wanted to understand the renegade, the sell-out, the Judas, in short.

"A little fellow. Needless to say, Jewish. Black hair and a dark complexion and such dark, Russian moods. His hands wrapped in each other behind his back as he walked solitary down all your streets, his jaw jutting out, and his eyes and ears poised to spring upon a street music that would justify his pain—a cough! A cough at night and he would think that

the whole world was in pain. And if it were a child's cough!
—More tea?"

Victoria brought her wrist watch into the light.

"Yes, thank you."

"Lemon?"

A nod.

"We met when we were freshmen. We were in the same
class and were the bright ones. He would stare at me as if
to discover in my face my history, my thoughts, everything. One day, after class, he demanded we go for a cup of
coffee. Seated, he said—I paraphrase—, 'All right. What do
you want to be? to do? to see?' Well, we spoke of god,
communism, James Joyce, and, of course, of the novels
Max was to write.

"But the novelist has become, or so it seems, novelist
manqué. I can well imagine why. The disesteem of the un-
published novelist once denied the title of student must
have been hard for him, so proud and poor, to bear. And
Academe with its halls of ivy must have appeared to him a
haven, a place where he might have respect as well as time
to continue his writing. Ah, the dreamer! For who in
Academe has time for serious work?

"Smiling, Vickie?"—with a small smile.

"His pain, however, was real and his loneliness was not
self-imposed or the cause of some 'internal disturbance.'
Both parents had died pathetically, the drawn-out suffering
of slow and incurable malignancies, and he, poor fellow, at
the side of each with hardly a year's respite between deaths
. . ."—continuing daringly— ". . . the pain communicated
into each and every nerve, holding the hand of his father
and then his mother who would not let him go . . ."

Victoria stood. "It's very late," she said.

She retrieved her bamboo umbrella, supple, handsome,

her favorite of ten, glanced quickly at Edgar, her great grey eyes, so sensitive to dust, her chiefest attraction of many, glaring.

Edgar followed her to the door, pleased that he had so affected her. "Tonight at nine?"

She did not reply and was gone, elegant with umbrella.

Victoria's apartment was on the twenty-seventh floor of a Riverside Drive building. There were five rooms, the main room large enough to be called a hall. The view from the hall was remarkable at sunset; the window was twelve feet wide and eight feet high and it faced, across the Hudson River, the New Jersey Palisades. The sun sank behind the palisades at a level, it seemed, with the apartment, and the hall, like the sky, became suffused with a rich, dark light. Nor was the view at night very much less fine. To the right, a bit north, the simply arched lines of the George Washington Bridge were outlined by lights; and almost directly below the apartment were automobiles on the West Side Drive, bodiless from up here, just lines of red and white light. Now and then, one could see the lights of a barge or freighter moving up or down river.

Guests entered the apartment at the head of a wide passageway the walls of which were hung with old framed maps, lithographs, sketches, small watercolors, were divested of hats and portables by Victoria's Jamaican maid and directed up the passageway—seeing the palisades at the end of the passageway as if it gave on to them, or, at night, seeing in the window the dark but clear reflections of themselves and of people and objects in the hall not yet otherwise in view.

The center portion of the hall floor was covered by a heavy, richly dark woven silk rug. A grand piano, its lid nearly always raised, was off to a side of the large window—the only window. An off-white chaise longue, the wood painted gold, flaking, was on the other side of the window, only further into the hall, dominating the center of the hall. A sofa, some tables and small armchairs were here and there, one evening forming two areas off the center of the hall, another placed discreetly by the walls. One large side wall was nearly entirely hidden by books, phonograph records, speakers—the books including the kind of art collection that is built over a long time, in new and old and yellowing editions. On the other side wall was a handsomely framed copy, about a half of the original's size, of the Botticelli "Birth of Venus."

It was in the hall that the Wolgamuts held their evenings.

This evening, the Fall semester not yet having begun, and certain of the Wolgamuts still out of the city, those present in addition to Victoria were Donald Marwel, Miss Jane Robinson, and Chester Mawr.

The first of these, Donald Marwel, Associate Professor of English at Y, was a well-known and highly regarded poet. He was forty, tall, a bit stout, with a large seat which he called his "writer's growth." His wife, Emily, generally in attendance at Wolgamut evenings, was presently visiting in New England.

The second, Jane Robinson, nineteen years old, a student, had been first brought to a Wolgamut evening by Donald and Emily, Donald's discovery through the journal Jane Robinson had been obliged to write for Donald's composition class. He thought her a talented and sensitive writer. She was tall and thin. She generally wore blue jeans and boys' button-down shirts; her long black hair was forever falling across her forehead, getting in her eyes—she was forever pushing it away like brushing away flies. For all that, she was very handsome. Many people called her Robinson; Victoria called her Jane; and Chester Mawr called her, with some irony, Miss Robinson.

Chester Mawr was fifty-five, a professor of English at Y, an authority on Elizabethan ballads who neatly separated his teaching and scholarship from his other activities, occasionally writing articles during the day, and enjoying New York in one way or another nearly every evening. He was a bachelor, a dear friend of Victoria with whom he often went to lunch, to the theater or a concert. He was short, pink-skinned, and round in all his parts.

These three were seated cross-legged on cushions on the silk rug playing Monopoly with Victoria when Edgar, not insensible to the hurt he had caused Victoria earlier in the day, arrived with a dozen white roses in hand.

They greeted Edgar from the floor.

He, with fine gallantry, bowed his roses to Victoria. She bowed her head maidenly in turn, and then left her place in the game to Edgar while she went to accommodate the flowers.

"A peace offering?" Donald Marwel inquired good-naturedly.

"Is it not?" Edgar replied. "Vickie and I are never fully at war or fully at peace, but we are always offering war and offering peace. The happiest kind of romance. Not so, Chester?"

The round man, the most urbane of the Wolgamuts, smiled no more than politely.

Donald, by a raised eyebrow, indicated to Edgar that all was not well between Robinson and Chester.

So the game was the thing.

Victoria returned. The white roses were arranged with sprigs of heather in an earthen vase.

Edgar quoted: *"How but in custom and ceremony*
    Are innocence and beauty born?"

He offered Victoria her place, but she chose not to play and settled herself above the game in her chaise longue.

"Marvin Gardens, Miss Robinson?"

She shook her head.

"Come, come, Miss Robinson. I'll take Marvin Gardens off your hands and you can have the B & O and the Pennsylvania lines."

She shook her head a second time.

"Edgar, dear boy, Miss Robinson thinks I am a nasty old man and for that reason will have nothing to do with me. But you will not let prejudice (or should I say naked truth?) stand in the way of sound commerce. You may have my two railroads for Park Place."

A trade was made.

"You see, Miss Robinson," Chester resumed, "some people would be hurt were a charming person like yourself to take a sudden dislike to them. But I feel there is little malice in your dislike, knowing as I do the excessive impressionability of the young."

"I don't dislike you," Robinson said, unable to face him.

"That is already something! And do you promise not to reveal my little secret?"

She nodded.

"Then, having your word, I shall confess my failing to the others. I was seen by Miss Robinson late one night or early one morning caressing—I believe that is the word—the hand of a young gentleman whose name, none of you being familiar with, you will surely excuse my not mentioning. Ah, Miss Robinson, look about you. No look of shock meets the eye. Perhaps I detect a bit of pity, of amusement, worst of all, a bit of boredom. We all have our little vices, Miss Robinson, and you will do well to learn not to frown on another's lest someone pry into your own. Edgar, will you be so kind as to put one house on Boardwalk and another on Park Place?"

In the big window, Victoria saw the reflections of the players, and, staring hard, made out between faces and furniture the New Jersey lights, everything less than real in and through her window, reflections and vistas imposed one on the other like screens light as gauze.

She said, "Well, everyone will soon be back and what shall we do?"

None of the players answered, either enmeshed in the game or not understanding the question.

"We might play bingo," Victoria suggested caustically.

Donald and Robinson left together; Chester left a few minutes later.

Victoria's maid arranged the Monopoly set in its box and put it away. Before she left the hall, she switched off all the lamps but one, in a corner, which, throwing most of its force up the raised lid of the piano, left Victoria and Edgar—he seated in an armchair facing Victoria on the chaise longue—mainly in shadows, lost in the size and obscurity of the room.

Edgar studied Victoria and with patient pleasure. There was grace to her every posture, every move; she did everything so seemingly naturally and artlessly that it was art itself. He felt very settled in his chair. He set to cleaning his pipe and said, "Robinson enters upon the night. I wonder less at her reaction to Chester's indiscretion than at the fact that she was a witness to it. Alone was she? And the night has its attractions. Had I, for example, not met you, I'd surely now be jobless, a rover, a nighttime character, and not because it's in my nature to be so, but because it's not in my nature—just as it's not in yours—to study halfway marks. That didn't come to pass. I'm in your apartment, in your company, in your most delightful web. The night, the strange fruits of which you'll never know—of living on the city street, of searching for sensations, for humiliations—is closed to me."

Victoria was watching him with a small smile.

He said, "I've known such characters as I might have become. Alex. He'd stand drunk but straight at the entrance of the College Bar and to each person he could stop, he'd say, 'Listen, I'm broke and I've got no place to sleep. Put me up for the night, will you? I'll sleep on the floor, in the bathtub.' Pausing then as if he had posed not a beggar's demand but the question of Christian charity, he'd stare brutally into the eyes of his pupil. He lacked no wit, that one! For I'd reach into my pocket and give him a dollar, which performance would be re-enacted all through the night by other students gentle enough not to want that wine-red wino on their floors, and gentle enough to feel guilty enough to buy him and his question off with a dollar or a quarter. He was a philosopher. Perhaps he had no answers, but he posed the questions: Shall we kiss the leper? Of course not—we build a colony in the Pacific to house him. Trust me, Victoria, the night has its most stellar attractions."

He laughed softly. He continued. "You take a person and keep him up all night on city streets and he'll do something he'll be ashamed of in the morning. But in the morning—isn't it so?—he's another person.

"Chester too appreciates the night, and like the best of us, hides his nighttime transactions under darkness and a word—caress! Caress, indeed. The mind is soothed by the word; it rests with the image of a hand resting lightly on another. But the word is a lie, a comforting one. And so we live, many of us, comforting ourselves with caresses. Good that way! Can you imagine what we'd be like were we to have no words like caress, no masks, manners, and all (I am but half-ironic) those good things?"

He paused but Victoria did not choose to reply.

"Watch Robinson. She'll be our case study."

"Mister Edgewater," Victoria said mockingly.

"Edgewater?"

"You stand by the seaside and make your most scientific observations."

"What would you have me do?" He asked lightly. "Caress affection from reason? Involvement from observation?"

She would not answer.

He studied her as if to read her mind. He would have risen and approached her but that he was afraid of awkwardness. He said instead, looking away, "Sometimes, I admire Alex for his honesty."

"Oh, Alex. You speak of him as if, 'what a jolly person to be and that's what I would have been.' But let me remind you that that's not what you were. Yes, you were a bit seedy, you were rude, but, my dear, you wore a tie. In fact, your 'no halfway mark for me' was no more than an edge-water mark. Oh, perhaps you put your feet in up to the ankles, and there you stood, waiting for someone to pull you out."

"And you appeared like Nausicaa?" he asked laconically.

"You think I found you attractive? Perhaps. Perhaps I thought it would be amusing to, well, to restore you. Perhaps I thought of it as a little game. Or perhaps I was tired of games and wanted something a bit different. Well, I did my searching in shallow waters and fished an edgewater."

"Sorry?"

"Am I not?" she asked.

He smiled even as she.

2

Jane Robinson liked to be in the company of children—moody, handsome boys or girls between the ages of six and eleven. Then, they were most beautiful, most alone, so much in their own world. Adults rarely pleased Robinson. For her, the world was divided into children and adults and the adults were all corrupt.

Yet, here she was, nineteen years old.

Every month, her parents—her father a well-to-do lawyer in Youngstown, Ohio—sent her a two hundred dollar allowance, this in addition to her tuition, room and board which they paid for at the beginning of each semester. Robinson would have liked to give the money to a beggar, a blind man, an amputee, or even to a drunk, but she could not bring herself to give away what was hers and yet was not, thinking that once she had given it away, she would have made a decision, chosen a way of life—to live for others, to live forever weeping for the blind and lame, ridiculed by everyone, and, forever removed from something she cherished even as much as her sympathy for others— that she could not forgive the world for being what it was. So, each month, upon receipt of her parents' check, she presented herself at a different savings bank in jeans and dirty white raincoat and opened a new account, pitting herself, she thought, against the bank, hoping that in the course of the formalities the bank would turn her out, say, "No, you won't do." But, with two hundred dollars, she always did do.

Changes began to occur. For a period, she lost control over most practical affairs. She was often late for class, fell feverish just at the time of examinations, was late in returning to the dormitory at night and was consequently locked out to spend the night wandering the streets. If she had to pick up her laundry, she had surely lost her laundry ticket; she paced twenty minutes in front of the shop before getting up the courage to enter and say, not, "I lost my ticket," but hopelessly, "Please trust me, I lost my ticket." She retreated more and more into silence and the journal she kept for Donald Marwel's composition class.

And Donald Marwel cultivated her, adopted her.

What the well-known poet saw in her, she could not understand. She hated her prose for being false; she hated her face, her long, thin body. She was always nervous; her hands perspired; she bit her nails and picked at them, one nail grating against another in a hand almost a fist. And yet, Donald clearly liked her. He encouraged her visits; he gave her novels and poetry to read; and he never tried to take advantage of her. He calmed her a bit, enough for her to

do better in school work, for her to observe others more
than she had. Among the Wolgamuts, she listened to every
word spoken, watched every gesture as if to learn to dupli-
cate it, even though she distrusted, except for Donald,
every one of them.

Robinson wondered if Donald wanted to change her, or
was it that he was interested in studying her? In any event,
she came to have a certain confidence in him—he was so
nice. In conversation as in poetry, he rarely spoke of the
bad in people, but esteemed the good. Nor had he, it
seemed to Robinson, cut himself off from the world as had
the other Wolgamuts. He courted experience—meeting
new people, visiting areas of the city, attending events; he
went to watch famous political and religious leaders just as
he went to Coney Island or Roseland—to observe, to com-
pare and to know. At times, Robinson thought that Donald
walked through experience like a phantom, bodiless and
untouched. At other times, she thought he was a sort of
Buddha, knowing so much and so quiet. Nothing he saw
could ruffle his mild manner. The worst of what he saw
produced in him a mild, "Ah, they should know better."

This summer, during the absence of Donald's wife, Emily, Robinson accompanied the poet on many of his excur-
sions and was introduced by him to people she recognized
as important. She could but infrequently overcome her fear
of speaking—these were all published men and who was
she. She sometimes wore a skirt, once or twice she put on
lipstick, but she could not get the lipstick on just right, nor
would her hair stay in place. Some of the men she met with
Donald took her aside and invited her to stay the night.
Once or twice she accepted, in handsome, carpeted, midtown apartments, with the phonograph going and a Monet
reproduction over the low, modern sofa where the pub-

lished man made his play. She would neck wildly but would go no further; attracted to her own fall, she teased it, and consoled herself later with her entries in her journal, writing in that book as if she were preparing a charge sheet against Man.

One summer evening, Robinson went with Donald to a party in Greenwich Village. Donald was taken off to a corner by the host who was flattered he had come. Robinson, in jeans, her hair nearly covering a side of her face, was uncomfortable, hot and perspiring in the press of talking, drinking, smoking people none of whom she knew. She made her way through them to the bedroom and climbed out the window to sit on the fire-escape, sandwiched there in semi-darkness between two buildings, five flights up, with only a sliver of the street in view. She smoked a cigarette; her eyes focussed on the glowing tip. She heard the party noises, the street noises, and was content to be so close and so removed from everything going on. She sat that way several minutes and was suddenly uneasy. She turned to the window and drew in her breath sharply. A bearded man was framed in the window not three feet from her, regarding her, sipping a drink. She turned quickly away and staring at a dirty building wall saw the man still. He was tall, lean; he wore a faded red shirt; his beard was black. His eyes were tired, indifferent—more tired than anything she had ever seen. She thought he was drunk and that was all right. She was too timid to look at him. She dropped her cigarette and watched it tumble all the way to the ground; over and under; it hit a fire-escape railing and swung out in a last arc. He sat down beside her.

"Luther," he said.

She followed his lead. "Robinson."

"You with Marwel?"

She nodded.

After a moment, he said, "It figures."

"What figures?"

"Nothing figures."

He lit a cigarette.

"You want to go to my place?"

She shook her head.

"Getting much?"

She did not understand.

"The least you can do is get me a drink."

She did. When she returned, he was gone.

She looked down, her heart pounding. She saw only shadows.

She returned to the party and looked everywhere for Luther. Donald was still with the host. She heard the host use the expressions "zeitgeist," and "essential sanity" in talking about Donald's poetry. An ugly little man whose every word was oil and whose beady eyes kept searching for a weakness. He threw in, "Your *Letter to My Wife* resembles just a bit a poem by . . ." But let the attack die because Donald met all his words with the same mild comments and mild smile.

Robinson hesitated to address the host, but then, unthinking, brushed her hair back and using a tone of Victoria Harm asked, "Have you seen a certain Luther?"

The tone was not enough to save her from a smile.

"You mean Luther Halverson. Was he here?"

Robinson nodded.

The host explained to Donald: "A writer of sex stories or sex mystery stories, he just appears and disappears. No one knows where he lives, no one invites him, he just comes and drinks, and sometimes fights, brawls, and then drives off, generally with a broad, in a run-down Jaguar. I tried to speak to him once. Well, he put his hands on his hips and listened to me for a minute, and then, as if he didn't know what he was doing, he stepped on my toe, not hard, just gently, but then began to press, hoping, I bet, that I'd start a fight. He's a commercial, a fascist-type, maybe even a paranoid, a failure who wants to be thought interesting."

After that evening, what could Robinson think but that Luther Halverson, like her, was outside all groups, a loner in a world of cliques and phonies?

She saw him in a Village "black and tan" place she had first gone to with Donald. He was with a handsome col-ored girl. The place was crowded, ill-lit. Robinson maneu-vered to a position just a few feet from him. She heard snatches of speech: "No kidding." "You don't say." Each word he spoke flattened by an indifference that was almost, Robinson thought, contempt. She left unseen, feeling very alone—alone on the narrow, noisy, Village streets; sad, her hands dug into the pockets of her raincoat, and suddenly, she stopped before a parked sports car she knew had to be Luther's: a world-weary, low, black Jaguar—old, dusty, the black leather upholstery dry and cracking.

One morning at two, she saw the car parked outside of North Ten, a cheap Village coffee place. She wrapped her raincoat tightly about her and entered the place, her eyes downcast. She found a stool at the counter. "Coffee," she mumbled to the waiter. Luther was seated two stools away from her, looking at her exactly as he had when she had been on the fire-escape. Robinson grew pale. She met his gaze, glancing down, but always back to him, wondering in a panic of thought what he saw, what he was thinking, searching in his tired eyes for just a touch of feeling.

"Robinson?"

She smiled as openly as a child that he remembered her name.

"Hi," she said.

"You were with Marwel?" he asked.

She nodded, her eyes downcast, fighting to keep her hands from her mouth, to face him like an equal.

He said, "That's all right. Marwel's a good poet, the very best. You at college?"

She nodded.

"Want to come along?"

"With the big bad wolf?" She dared.

"Like you don't have to," he said.

He paid his bill.

Robinson paid her own and followed him out.

She stood waiting until he, seated low in his car, gestured her to get in. They drove to his apartment west of the Village, almost at the river. It was the middle of the night, but the river area was alive with lights and noise. Thirty-ton trucks were being discharged by crews of bare-backed, sweat-streaked workers, by machines that groaned and crawled their way into truck trailers. From Luther's second floor apartment, Robinson heard the roar of the ever-moving trucks, machines, traffic.

The noise, dirt, heat of the street were all there in Luther's apartment, caught there like dirt in a crack. The apartment consisted of one room, a tiny kitchen and a bathroom. The few articles of furniture were cast-off things, an over-stuffed armchair. The bed had been pushed to lie beneath the open window and was unmade, the linen unclean. A small table with upright typewriter and a pile of manuscript on it was by the bed, so that one could type from the bed.

Robinson sat in the armchair.

She looked up and Luther was standing above her, waiting. Her hand went to her mouth; she tore at a nail. She spoke to the wall: "I want to write. I want to write so bad it hurts. I want to write of everything I feel and how rotten everything is. It's so dirty here! Don't you ever clean?" She glanced up and then away, like something trapped. "But you're right to live here. I've walked here. At night. Alone. And men follow me. They follow me until I want to run. They think I'm a prostitute. I can tell from the way they look at me. They have such ugly faces I want to laugh. You live like a spider here, don't you?" And again she looked up and then away. "Maybe if you made enough money, you could take time to write something good. But maybe you don't want to, just don't want to put anything down because how can you? The moment you write it out, it's gone, and you're in another world, the very world, and people criticize your art and art has nothing to do with it. It's me. It's me that's on paper. 'Just add a line here, Robinson. Perhaps you might develop this thought, Robinson?' Can't I stay the night with you? And in the morning, we'll clean the apartment and I'll make breakfast."

She was in his arms, kissing him, re-kissing him, and french-kissing him. He removed her raincoat, edged her around the table to the bed, eased her down upon it, all without breaking the embrace. She was prone, her eyes were closed; she thought she was falling and she wanted it, but she broke from him and sat up and found herself looking into the street. The street lamps were almost on a level with her; she saw the dirty little buildings opposite like the one she was in. She heard the roar of the trucks; she shuddered; his arms had encircled her and his fingers were at the buttons of her shirt. He removed her shirt; he unclipped her bra. She wished someone would pass and that she would be seen as she was, her small young breasts bare, in the window.

He went to the bathroom.

He returned naked. She turned quickly to the window, crossing her arms over her breasts. He switched off the light and lay down at her side.

He asked her if she wanted to take off her jeans.

She rushed from the bed, stood with her back to him on the other side of the table. In the light and shadows of the room, her back was pale and boyishly slender. She said, "I'm virgin."

She waited. He said nothing.

"Getting much?" she asked, turning then with a small, nervous smile.

He came to her—white, spectral. She felt his hands pressing her to him, the breadth of his hands covering all the expanse of her back. She kissed him as before, violently, variously. She began with her lips and tongue to play with his lips and tongue, touching and withdrawing, her hands behind his ears, fingertips caressing.

He was once again edging her around the table. She was familiar with the direction but she let him do as he wished. He eased her down upon the bed and his hands went to her jeans, trying to open the metal buttons. Her eyes were wide open. She stared at the ceiling through a film of tears. He saw she was crying and he lay down on his back.

Leaning on her elbow, looking down at him, Robinson said, now teasing his beard, now his eyes, "There are cat people and dog people and the cat people live by night and don't need anyone." Her hand was on his body, tracing lines here and there. "And we're both cat people."

She asked, "Do you have something to drink?"

He nodded, indicating vaguely a corner of the room.

She got off the bed, found a nearly empty bottle of gin and took it with her to the bathroom. She sat on the edge of the bathtub and drank from the bottle. She drank again and for a little while felt sick. She switched on the light and looked at herself in the medicine chest mirror. She held the bottle to her lips, looking at herself. She wished she had a lipstick. She took off her jeans and then her little pants and posed for herself, unable to see all of herself until, ashamed, she went out of the bathroom to Luther, and, like a child, nuzzled her head under his chin.

She lay on her back and let him do what he wanted.

Later, he said, "I thought you said you were virgin?"

Staring at the ceiling, she said, "I was."

He said nothing. She turned to look at him. His eyes were closed; he was breathing lightly, regularly.

She repeated, "I was."

It was late in the morning. She awoke with the sun full on her face. She heard the city noises, recognizing after a minute the sound of trucks, of cars, voices on the street below. Had it been darker, quieter, she would have kept her eyes tightly closed and built a dream. But the light was in her closed eyes yet. She remembered what had passed and that Luther had not believed her. And even before she opened her eyes a second time, a half-smile formed on her lips, she thinking of yesterday's Robinson, of saying to her, "Sure, I believe you."

She leaned on her elbow and studied Luther asleep at her side. Coolly, patiently, regarded him from head to toe. His body was covered by dark little hairs, and yet was pale in the light, almost sickly pale compared to her own. She thought her breasts had grown in the night; the nipples of his were small and hard. She looked from one triangle of hair to the other. She was about to cry; her hand went involuntarily to her mouth and she bit on the side of her thumb. To cover herself. To close her eyes and dream. Luther was sleeping so lightly, she thought she could tease him awake with a single caress.

She saw, nearly hidden by his beard, a little mark like a cold sore at the corner of his mouth, the spot of flesh cracked and rotten. She touched it gently, pityingly, half-smiling all the while into Luther's face as if it were Luther and not she who had, several hours earlier, wanted to be believed.

Suddenly, she sat up. She woke Luther, shaking him by the shoulder.

"Isn't there something I should do?"

He covered his eyes with his arm. When he understood, he told her to look in the medicine chest.

She found an ugly device there. She stood holding it. He was in the doorway, looking at her. His gaze, for the first time, was almost kind. She stared fixedly down at the device. He told her how to use it and left her. She used it and, as if she had been given a badge, she felt a certain satisfaction.

Robinson dressed and going again to the bathroom, hid the device in her raincoat to take back with her to the dormitory. Parting, she asked Luther when she would see him again. He said whenever she liked and kept on typing.

Afterwards, they saw each other frequently.

Robinson often carried the device about with her. She

bought a big, black, expensive Italian shoulder bag for it. She liked the idea that it was so expensively covered. Even when she wore jeans, the shoulder bag gave her a jaunty, professional look, like a model going to work.

3

One evening, shortly before the beginning of the Fall semester, Edgar Hope dined alone at the Boston, a small restaurant on Broadway in the university area. There was room for about forty and during the school year it was crowded at meal times and only a bit less so all through the afternoon when steady clients, among whom figured many of Edgar's acquaintances, came for long coffees, filling the place with smoke and talk. Edgar ate there often, as he had ever since he had first come to the university. This evening, the restaurant was nearly empty, the proprietor at the front, leaning on his cash register, looking into the street.

Edgar was sipping his coffee and studying a *Cue* magazine—searching for old Fred Astaire or Katherine Hepburn films, circling some titles for a later and final selection—

when Max Wise entered the restaurant. Edgar recognized him immediately and stood and spoke his name.

The Russian scholar clasped Edgar's hand in both of his.

He was six inches shorter than Edgar; he had grown just a bit stout. He was dressed well, carelessly. His eyes were black, intense—as they had been—demanding, one might say, mocking, another might say.

They sat down together.

Edgar congratulated Max on his appointment as assistant professor.

And Max then launched into a description of his struggle to have his thesis accepted. He spoke the intellectual's language, but salted it with gestures of the street, sly smiles, warm looks, laughter. He had refused, he said, to make revisions, concessions, had had to fight with his doctoral committee. Edgar sat back, smiling with pleasure, thinking that Max was the kind of person to encourage open enmities, and Edgar did not know another person like that. That Max had had to push his way forward, fighting for every step. Max recounted the breaks which had finally begun to come his way: chapters of his thesis had been published here and there; a university press was going to publish the whole; and then had come the offer from Y. Edgar pictured Max in some mid-western university town receiving the letter, taking it to his department chairman and asking him to meet this offer, asking just for the pleasure of watching the chairman's face, for Y was New York and the end of exile.

Max spoke about the city, his city, so changed, so unchanged, only more so; he spoke about his bad luck in finding an apartment. He said he could not stomach living in a project and that what he wanted, and he could afford it, was—with a wink—a bachelor's apartment. "But you?"

he abruptly inquired.

"Oh me," Edgar said with some nonchalance. But, as Max continued to regard him, he said, "Very little. No publications, no offers, no tenure."

"It'll come," Max said, smiling just the same.

He ordered his dinner.

He asked, "Your thesis?"

"It takes time. Theories of Aesthetics in Jane Austen."

"Fine. You might, as a side issue, talk about morality in her work. How she really detests every convention she celebrates. Including marriage."

"Dear Max, I don't allow myself the psychoanalytic approach."

"Every time you dear Max me, I know you're in trouble. But never mind. We'll talk Jane Austen another time. Tell me something about yourself."

"What can I tell? I've been here ever since I returned from England. Some summers abroad. I live, as you'll surely discover, on the surface of things."

"That," Max said, "I already know."

"Really?"

"Luther keeps me informed," he said, smiling.

Edgar reddened just a bit. He said, "Is he then in the employ of the FBI?"

"Nothing so cynical. I'm staying with him. Shall we visit him?"

"As a matter of fact, I shall be busy this evening."

"With Miss Harm?"

"No, dear Max, with Miss Hepburn."

Max laughed. He said, "No, no, you'll come with me and we'll talk of old times. We'll tell old stories. We'll reminisce with Luther, though frankly, it's hard to talk with him. We might not even be welcome. I've been there a week and he's a busy man—social commitments and all that—and maybe he's beginning to find me in his way. Anyhow, he's the writer. Cheap little books. And me? I don't write. No, don't look sad. I discovered I had no imagination. Really. But when it comes to people I know, I've a fairly good imagination. You know the secret? Look at the person and imagine the worst. The absolute worst. Lucid. You become lucid that way."

"You're a funny little man."

Max laughed. He said, "I'd forgotten."

"Pardon?"

"I'd forgotten that expression, 'little man.'"

"Have I used it before?"

"You're really admirable," Max said affably. "Anyhow," he said after a moment, "while I eat, tell me about Miss Harm."

"You know so much already."

"Victoria, isn't it?"

"She's twenty-five, well-educated, well-traveled and, I would say, very attractive. But you'll meet her soon enough. You'll come to one of our evenings. You've heard, no doubt, of the Wolgamuts."

"Edgar," Max remonstrated gently, "you haven't told me a thing about your Victoria."

"What, exactly, would you like to know?"

"The worst."

"Ah, the worst."

They sat smiling at each other, Max engaged with his food, an expert carver, separating nerve from meat neatly. Edgar forced himself to laugh.

"Do you sleep with her?" Max asked casually.

"A typical Max question."

"A typical Edgar response. I assume you do not. And how much money does she have?"

"I'm afraid I never asked."

"And yet, even your Jane Austen lists incomes. Such details, you know, make for the whole. So come now, search in your memory and give me a detailed picture of your beloved. You love her, don't you?"

"Who should say?"

"Then you don't love her. When will you marry?"

Edgar smiled for answer.

"Shall we try again? Do you sleep with her?"

"You are tedious."

Max regarded Edgar patiently, smiling. He said: "I never know with you whether you're a fool (no, don't be offended, it's just a way of speaking, for even if you were a fool, it'd be for some noble reason) or whether you're an Englishman. You know what I mean? Stiff upper lip. Only the stiff upper lip tends to become a smile—the triumph less in keeping your pathetic little secrets all to yourself than in the smile. See, I've read your friend Marwel's poetry. Nothing has meaning for him until it sits down to breakfast with him and his wife. Death too. Death sitting down to breakfast with Mr. and Mrs. Marwel. 'Say hello, dear. Our guest is a great voyager and has much to tell us. Smile, dear.' No. Let me tell you about your Victoria. Facts. First: rich—there's a fifty-fifty chance she's Episcopalian. Second: well-traveled—she's been five times to Italy, recently to Japan. She's tired of the renaissance; she prefers the romanesque. Third: well-educated—she, if she doesn't sleep with you, sleeps with another. At the very least, she masturbates."

"Max, you're wonderful."

"A wonderful little man?"

"A wonderful little man. What should I ever do without you?"

"Flounder."

"But will you tell me who is Luther's informant?"

"That would be indiscreet. Besides, perhaps Luther will tell you himself."

They taxied to the Village. Luther was not at home.

The apartment was in disorder. A mattress lay on the floor in a corner by the radiator; the sheets were more grey than white as were those on the bed by the window. Edgar walked about as was his habit whenever he entered an unfamiliar apartment, looking for books, objects, but found nothing to interest him. The furnishings were Salvation Army; everything was dusty; he would have preferred to stand.

Max served gin.

Edgar sat down in the armchair; Max sat on Luther's bed.

"If you want another place," Edgar said, "you can move in with me until you find an apartment."

"You're kind."

"It's my nature to be so."

Max established that Edgar had not heard of Luther since Luther had begun at law school. He said that Luther, tempestuous of spirit, had been early expelled from there. For some minor infraction—like failing each and every of his courses. He had not ever—that was evident—seriously thought of the law as a career, or, perhaps he simply had never considered the three additional years of school, the study of torts. A defender of the downtrodden, he had considered the effect and never the form of his defense.

Then, Jack London to a fault, he had worked in a cannery, as a lumberman . . .

"You kept up with him all this time?"

"Letters. Occasional meetings. Chicago. New Orleans."

"And after?" Edgar asked. "He began to write?"

"He worked on ships," Max said. "He saw the world. Returning from one trip, he had a bit of cash and found himself in the Village. Greenwich. He was twenty-five or six. He liked a beer and a drink and other things he had picked up a taste for in the course of his wanderings. He went Villagey—hating the place, sticking to it. He bought a typewriter . . ."—Max pointed to the upright—". . . and said to himself, 'Why not me?' Not, why not me, James Joyce, but, why not me, George Harmon Coxe. And he sold. Commercial stuff—tales his grandfather had told him of the great north, written with verve and sold to *Verve*. He struck out for bigger fields. One, if one knows how, can make a tidy sum from a mystery. Sex. Violence. Why he was right at home.

"Anyhow, they're pretty bad baggage, his books. And the one he's doing now is so rotten he can't even finish it. He's been working on it—working, did I say?—more than a year. And money, by the way, doesn't grow on trees."

Edgar was strangely pleased by Max's account. Perhaps perversely that Luther, like himself, had suffered or was suffering an *échec*. It pleased him too that Luther was in "it" up to his neck. It was almost enough to make him willing to forgive Luther for having been in the city so long and never having tried to get in touch. But, it was perhaps not enough to forgive him for speaking behind his back. And it occurred to him that Max and Luther had perhaps sat here, speaking of him and laughing at him.

4

Late in the summer, Robinson showed her journal to Donald Marwel. Each journal entry until now had been prefaced only by the date; now, all were dateless and some were prefaced *Dear Buddha*. At first, Donald thought that the new preface was the result of a literary influence, but then, as he read the entries, he very quickly understood that he was Buddha and that the journal entries were written if not for him then at him.

Dear Buddha: I'll call him the catman because he's like a cat—dark and quick and indifferent and he lives by night. He's tall and lean and hardly speaks at all, and I'm curled up on his bed, watching him NOT-write. He's written five or six books, cheap things, but they do have a plot, a story, and everything was invented while he was at the typewriter, just right off the top of his head. And for each book, he got three thousand dollars. I can see how he works—maybe sitting at the typewriter twelve hours a day for a week, or two weeks, and then, there's a book. But I think he's getting tired now. He writes maybe twenty pages in two or three hours, but then he throws them out and starts all over again, from scratch. Sometimes, I think he'd like to bang his fists against the key of the typewriter and stamp out a book. A thousand books in his head. And sometimes I think he's bored by his work and more than anything, he likes to watch his fingers fly over the typewriter keys.

I'm curled up on the bed. He doesn't mind if I play the radio.

I asked him if he liked me.

He wanted to know if I wanted him to like me.

I told him I wasn't sure.

Sometimes, when he can't work, he kills flies. He does it with his right hand. He sits at the typewriter and if a fly lands anywhere around him, he sneaks his hand behind it and then slam, he catches it. And then he makes a fist.

He wanted to do it another way. I said all right. But when I couldn't see his face, I got very frightened.

Sometimes, I feel myself all like velvet, soft as velvet, which is funny because I'm really boney all over. I think he likes to touch my skin.

He doesn't want to like me, but he does.

Dear Buddha: Have you ever smoked incense? It's more greenish than tobacco. And you have to roll it yourself—thin. When you start smoking, you have to stay with it. There's an art to it. You can look all greedy doing it, or, like the catman, you can do it all loose, all of you in the inhale. Sometimes, when the catman's smoked a bit, he talks.

He said that when he was in Mexico, he couldn't speak Spanish, just enough to take a taxi, but he went to Tepoztlán to write, where there were no Americans, and he really got lost. Lost, couldn't work, found himself just looking at things. He noticed that his beard was growing. He'd stand hours in front of the mirror, not moving at all, and he said he could see the hairs growing. He'd look at stones, at water. A leafy tree wouldn't do because if a breeze came along it would move too violently. He said he could see movement in a stone, but such slow movement, so infinitely slow that he'd never have to turn his eye even a millimeter to follow the movement. He thought that if he wanted to and if he kept on this way, he'd become invisible. Really invisible. That he wouldn't be able to see himself and that no one would be able to see him. He said that it was a great experience, the greatest and most frightening of his life. As if he had stood on the brink of the future. The real future. But then he laughed at himself and said that he would have been like Lamont Cranston, The Shadow.

I asked him if he believed in anything.
He sang me hymns to Jesus.
I said I believe in lights. Lights light the way.

I asked him if he'd like to write something good.
He said, "A Western. A big, short, simple Western."
"Why don't you?"
"I'm saving it."
"For what?"
"For a rainy day."

A Russian has come to stay. The Russian spoke about E. The catman knows E. They were once friends. But he doesn't care one way or the other about seeing him. I don't think he's happy to see the Russian either. Like maybe the Russian has a hold over him, maybe the catman owes him money. Anyhow, I don't think he likes him. I sit curled up on the bed. The Russian speaks about himself, all the time about himself no matter what he's talking about, and he's fat, not like the catman, and he's little, and I think he wants us to think he too's a cat, but he's not. Because he's so taken by himself, by his thoughts. He's all ego-intellectual like maybe some people are all pure-intellectual. Anyhow, he's ego-intellectual.

Since the Russian's come, we stay out a lot. Bars. Drives. The other night we were in the car. I asked him to let me drive. He said no. I don't think he wants me with him when he really drives. I think his car is his. I mean, he doesn't want anyone else to touch it. And I think he likes to drive fast and alone, all alone. Maybe I'll buy a car like his. We'll pass in the night, both going a hundred an hour, in opposite directions. Or maybe, we'll crash together.

I think he's suicidal.

He drove me to the dormitory. He does now and then. But never to the door, just to the university area, leaves me off by the Drive. This night, he got out with me and we went walking in the park and he became very sad, as if he'd walked there many times before. I asked him whom he'd gone walking with that he looked as if his best friend had died. He said that he'd walked there alone. We walked further. I wanted to run. So I began running and after a while, he ran too, with me, past trees, around trees, down through the park, toward the river which you could hardly see for the lights of the Drive. Then he left me behind, kept running all the way down to where the Drive cuts through the park and he didn't stop, but jumped the little fence and never lost his stride, almost flying across the Drive, and he missed smashing into a car by only a foot or two, not dodging—the driver never knowing what was happening—, but making it. I ran too, but I cheated in crossing, looking in both directions before I dashed into his arms, but was scared just the same in crossing, and he held me then and kissed me not sexy but brotherly. He was feeling all breathless, looking up, smiling at the sky, like maybe he enjoyed coming so close to getting killed.

Dear Buddha: What is a catman? A catman is free.

5

The evening of the first day of the new semester, the Wolgamuts gathered at Victoria Harm's apartment to play Edgar's new version of Monopoly on a wooden board six feet
square with seventy-two properties.

The handsomely marked heavy board was raised one
foot off the rug in the center of the hall; the players would
sit about the board, cross-legged on cushions. The hall was
everywhere well-lit; the large window was a near perfect
mirror, flawed here and there by a New Jersey light. And
in a corner of the hall, Victoria had had placed a portable
bar and had lettered on a piece of cardboard at its side:
TRADERS' BAR. It was here that the players would go to
"buy" each other drinks when they had a trade to make.

In addition to Victoria, Chester Mawr, Donald Marwel,

Robinson and Edgar, the Wolgamuts in attendance were Lucian Whittier, Charles Rizzo, Simon Parr, and Emily Marwel, the poet's wife. Also, Max Wise was there as Edgar's guest.

Lucian Whittier and Charles Rizzo were both Edgar's age and were Instructors at Y in the Fine Arts Department. Lucian was thick-lipped and baby-skinned, his cheeks soft, round and pink. He wore a pastel tinted shirt. "Winter pastel," he said, explaining his choice, smiling then in a sort of dare for he liked very much to discuss clothes and colors. Charles, on the other hand, was severely dressed; was lean, extremely dignified, handsome and pale.

Simon Parr, an Instructor in English at Y, was ascetic-looking; tall, cave-chested, his long face was always studiously sober; and his voice lacked all modulation as if he disdained to give a word more than its dictionary definition demanded for it.

Emily Marwel worked at a university library. She was the same age as her husband, but seemed—lined and wan— closer to fifty than forty. She was tall and thin; her red hair was dull and very dry as if she were just getting over an illness. Sometimes, in the midst of a conversation, she would fade out, stand an instant staring at nothing, hearing nothing.

Max was politely received by the Wolgamuts.

Victoria spent a minute with him.

"Isn't it strange," she said, "that every time I try to read Dostoevsky, I never get past page thirty?"

Max attempted to explain why.

She wore a fine knit beige dress; gold earrings; her hair was swept up. In heels, she was taller than Max; standing still, she was still in motion; smiling politely at him, her eyes nevertheless ranged here and there over the hall as if she had not the right to fully concentrate on one thing, but as hostess, had even while listening to him to think of this and that. Max was made to feel vaguely uncomfortable and he smiled wisely over his words as if he understood her perfectly.

Chester Mawr approached.

Victoria went off to talk with Charles.

"Haven't we met before?" Chester asked, his round body posed penguin-like before Max.

"I had a course in Elizabethan poetry with you."

"Ah!" Chester exclaimed with satisfaction.

But then said with seeming astonishment, "And went from that to Russian literature?"

Lucian Whittier said, "Why is it, Mr. Wise, that every time I start a Dostoevsky novel, I get bogged down by page one hundred?"

"I don't know you well enough to answer."

Lucian was tickled by the reply.

"I beg your pardon," Emily Marwel interrupted. She went on to tell Max—Lucian and Chester beginning a separate conversation, Donald approaching—that she had once started reading one of his articles but had not had the opportunity to finish it.

Max said that the article would soon be published in a book and he would see to it that she received a copy. He then addressed Donald, complimenting him on a recently published poem. He seemed delighted to speak with the poet, and he radiated charm. Donald, as always, let praise ride across his shoulders. His smile was disarmingly mild.

Edgar, keeping an eye on Max, began to wonder with

some amusement whether Max might not make himself a place at the Wolgamut table.

Robinson, also one of the evening's attractions—wearing as she did a dress, wobbly on heels—stood with Max. She called him by his first name as if they were already well-acquainted.

Charles Rizzo said to Max: "May I ask you sir, if you like your classes?"

"They seem to be just fine."

"Mine are not," Charles said. "But then, I teach two freshman courses. What I do is introduce them to some of the refinements of college life. For example, I inform them immediately that between Instructor and student there must always be a distance and that consequently the first two rows of seats must be left vacant. That is always an impressive moment—when they gather up notebooks and pens and disperse to the rear, some sheepishly, on tiptoe.

"But you, sir, I'm sure are a democrat."

Max nodded, mocking Charles with his eyes.

Edgar said, "Charles, you know, is our eccentric."

Max flashed Edgar a smile as if Edgar were a fool.

The game began.

Each of the players was given the equivalent of his yearly income in game money. Thus Robinson, who began with the sum given her and spent on her by her parents— four thousand five hundred dollars—was the game's poorest player and was at a disadvantage. The various other Wolgamuts entered the game with between six and fifteen thousand dollars, few of them not receiving in addition to their salaries small incomes from investments. Chester began with fifteen thousand dollars; he was followed by Edgar with five hundred dollars less. Donald Marwel began with eleven thousand, and Max Wise with seven thousand. Victoria acted as banker for were she to play the game on the same terms as the others, she would have far too great an advantage. She sat behind a table and sold properties. And, as an innovation, she administered loans at interest rates that varied, depending on her evaluation of the risks involved, between six and twenty percent—payable each time the debtor completed five full turns around the board.

Her table was placed near the GO corner of the board and she sometimes leaned a bit over it to watch the action below. She had several filing cards on which she recorded loans and interest payments; and the bank's funds were laid out at a side of the board in stacks of attractive bills with denominations of from one dollar to five hundred dollars.

Early in the game, Edgar acquired two green properties. Robinson had the matching third and fourth and Edgar, thinking to purchase them from her for fourteen hundred dollars—twice the sum she had paid for them—asked her to join him at the bar. There, she suggested that he sell her his two green properties for the same sum he had offered her. Edgar smiled and explained that were she serious—which he had his doubts about—and if he calculated well—which he had no doubts about—she would, purchasing his two greens, find herself very close to being without ready cash. Robinson said carelessly that Oh, she would arrange a loan. "And if it is refused, as who should say our banker will not refuse a loan to one so unfortunately impecunious as yourself?" But Robinson pleasantly if stubbornly held fast to her offer and Edgar finally agreed to it, expecting thereby to teach her a lesson.

Yet, a moment later, Edgar was surprised to see that Victoria did administer a loan to Robinson though, because Robinson, standing with her back to Edgar, was partially in his line of vision, he did not see for how much, nor hear at what interest rate. Buildings were already sprouting on the board; Chester controlled a five property monopoly and had sufficient funds to build hotels; Max controlled the railroads and "taking a ride" on any one of those six holdings cost three hundred dollars. Lucian and Emily already had monopolies. Had Victoria refused the loan and had Robinson, after her purchase, landed on certain of the monopolized properties, she would have been forced into mortgaging her holdings. Edgar realized that Victoria, with whom he had discussed in detail his innovations for the game and the principles behind the innovations, was doing no more than creating—as he had indicated she might— a companion variable to the dice, but just the same, he was irritated.

The other innovations were working more to his liking. The inequalities established by giving each player the equivalent of his yearly income was showing effects: Robinson was over-reaching herself; Chester, rich, played with a certain confidence; and Max, with less than half Chester's initial resources, had developed an imaginative game.

That one, Edgar thought, was a born trader. He understood the basic laws of making a Monopoly profit: trade with the weak; only when absolutely necessary reveal your real intention, otherwise, depending on whom you are dealing with, hint at one false or even several false intentions. Max, even as he had played a short-range game, gaining control of the railroads and thereby assuring himself a steady if slight income, had collected seemingly random properties, giving two blues for a railroad and "throw in a red and it's a deal." So that by the time he had collected the six railroads, he had traded off eleven properties, but had gained control of, in addition to the railroads, one red, one pink, one purple and one yellow property. Now it seemed that those properties might control the game.

It pleased Edgar to watch the dark little man—his own holdings, now that he had sold the greens, were too dull to interest him much. Max sat between Emily and Charles, close to the GO corner of the board, just beneath the banker's table. Smoking a great deal, smiling politely, he politely passed words with his neighbors, even with Charles, straight-backed, the two of them once or twice laughing, finding goodness knows what to talk about. Max, Edgar thought, was like a gambler who, aware of every card played, is yet able to give the impression that he is but carelessly involved in the game.

"Have you known him long?" Donald asked, standing at Edgar's side at the bar, nodding discreetly in Max's direction.

Edgar replied, speaking in the manner of Chester Mawr —rounding his phrases, each word gaining its fullest roundness at his lips: "We were college classmates and quite good friends, but I have not seen him in ten years and would say he had changed if not for the better, then not for the worse, leaving behind, shedding a skin, the image of him I have long maintained: walking alone on Broadway, his hands behind his back, suffering, serious, listening for a cough—the somber proof and reflection of his state of mind. A stage, no doubt, but at that time I found it attractive if romantic and thought it a way of life. But haven't you come across any of his work? For he has become a most competent scholar, and ambitious, preparing himself, I gather from a recent conversation, to 'tackle' Jane Austen."

Donald said that he had not read anything by Max and looked forward to doing so. He was smiling in his mild way and after having spoken a moment about Max's field and specialization, he inquired: "Has he been here long?"

"In New York?" Edgar asked, gaining time to study the poet's interest.

"I believe only a week or two."

"And would you know," Donald asked with some embarrassment, "if he knows a certain Luther?"

Simon Parr joined them.

The poet indicated to Edgar by a smile that they might resume their conversation later.

The tall and cave-chested new arrival arranged trades with both Donald and Edgar, each gaining possession of a first monopoly, and then began to speak about his summer spent in Greece.

Edgar stood back, looking on with polite interest.

Max had had news of him through Luther. Robinson knew Max. Was the link to Luther, Robinson or Donald? Had Robinson in her nighttime wanderings encountered more than Chester caressing the hand of one of his attachments? Edgar felt pricked then by anger and jealousy that he should be an outsider to his own circle.

Simon talked on. He had that remarkable ability that some scholars have of constructing even as he spoke not just his next sentence, but his next paragraph, page and chapter. Chapter One—Myths and Their Origins in the Greek Islands; subheadings—Myths and Patmos, Rhodes and Icaria.

Edgar wished he could pull in his little paunch, girdle himself against all doubts. Simon's future as a professor was surely better assured than his own. At the board, it was again his turn to throw the dice. He excused himself and returned there. Seated, he noticed that Robinson was flourishing. She had built three houses on each of the greens and had recently collected big rents.

Chester Mawr offered Max a considerable sum for his purple. Max countered that he would give him the property in exchange for twenty-five percent of all the revenue that might accrue to Chester through having the purple monopoly. He sub-conditioned with a smile, as if ashamed to mention it, that of course Chester, upon agreeing to the arrangement, would be obliged to build two houses on each of the purples. Chester smiled at Max's offer and firmly intended henceforth to ignore the intruder. He understood it was a seller's market, but assumed that the three other players who had reason to deal with Max (he looked now at Robinson, Charles and Lucian, estimating their strength of character, their financial resources) would follow his lead and look elsewhere for a second monopoly rather than submit to Max's outrageous terms. Assumed so and would have liked to close his mind to the subject, but, in spite of himself, kept thinking of the three players, that one or another would soon enough give in. He looked at Max Wise, recognizing in the dark-haired, consciously carelessly dressed man an interesting opponent. In any event, Chester thought, possessing a well-developed monopoly, he had nothing to fear, at least not for the moment. Then thought of Max even more respectfully—that the next time he asked for the purple, Mr. Wise would perhaps ask for thirty or forty percent. The round man smiled—if thinly, nevertheless with genuine amusement—at the new twist Mr. Wise had given the evening, smiled then in turn at each of Max's three other potential buyers, enjoying his own game of calculating which of the three would break ranks first.

Victoria beckoned to Edgar.

She had been counting the bank's funds, examining the filing cards on which she had recorded loans and interest payments, and had been jotting down figures which seemed, by her perplexed expression, not to have come out right. She stood as Edgar approached and they stepped back towards the window. She whispered, "I'm missing five thousand dollars."

"I don't understand."

"I think I do," Victoria said. "Somebody stole that money from the bank. Your friend is really a jolly specimen."

After a moment, Edgar asked, "Did you see him take the money?"

She shrugged impatiently. She asked, "Shall you do something, or shall you edgewater?"

"When did you first miss the money?"

"I counted it several minutes ago."

"And before?"

"It's the first time I checked."

"Was he ever at the table to make a loan?"

"Officer, he was right under the table all evening. All he had to do was reach up."

"Who has made loans?" Edgar insisted.

"You are pompous!"

"May I see the cards there?"

He took from the table the filing cards on which Victoria had recorded bank loans. He looked at one on which there was but one entry. He felt very strange and timid

with the proof in his hand and he really did not know what
to do. It was, after all, only a game.

"Well?"

"Well, it's not him."

"Who then?"

"I'm not sure," he said, putting her off.

Max invited Lucian to join him at the bar.

Max said that he was willing to let Lucian have the red
for a twenty percent concession instead of a twenty-five.
The Fine Arts Instructor asked Max why he was so generous. Max explained that such an arrangement would help
to tide him over until better days. Lucian smiled and asked
if it were not rather that he wanted to establish precedent.
Max smiled. Lucian said that he was one to always want to
establish precedent. But that he nevertheless still wondered
why Max had chosen him to make his bargain offer to.
Why not to Robinson? To Charles? Or even to Chester?
Was it not by a combination of financial reasons and moral
assumptions that he had narrowed the field to him? That he
posed no present threat and that he, Max assumed, would
have no scruples about dealing with him? Lucian seemed
delighted by his own logic. And he suggested that Max cut
another five percent from his offer, that he give him the red
for a fifteen percent concession.

When Max and Lucian returned to the board, Chester
said, addressing Edgar, "I think there is a question as to the
legality of Mr. Wise's proposition. What, for example,
would happen to his concession were Lucian to be, by
some misfortune, bankrupted?"

Edgar considered.

Max replied: "The fairest would be for me to be given

the option of buying the monopoly at seventy-five percent of the bank-declared value."

Lucian laughed.

Chester said, ignoring the Fine Arts Instructor, "And thus you would be binding all the players to a privately reached and unrecorded agreement. But plainly, an agreement can be binding on all the players only if it is agreed to by them."

"Unrecorded?" Max said.

"Omit 'unrecorded,' " Chester allowed.

Edgar was about to give judgment.

Max quickly put in: "Forget the option. Still, until my partner would be bankrupted, the agreement would concern only him and me. It's really no more than an extension of free landing privileges, and I can't see what's illegal about that."

Edgar said: "As long as you give up claim on the option, I think it's legal."

"In that case," Chester said, "what if some of us were to make an agreement not to have any dealings with Mr. Wise or anyone so mistakenly adventurous as to have dealings with him?"

"Bravo!" Lucian exclaimed.

"Legal too," Edgar said.

"Indeed legal! That way," Chester explained, "once Mr. Wise—excuse me, sir, for forever mentioning your name, but it's not with you personally that I take issue, but with the principle involved in your agreement—once Mr. Wise and his partner, the injudicious Lucian, are forced out of the game, as behind an effective embargo they will surely be, their properties will again be available at something less than black market prices."

Max leaned back, smiling under the prediction. He had

only so much cash and the revenues from his railroads and his concession would only with luck cover the rents he would pay in circling the board.

He asked Robinson, "Are you participating in this gentlemen's agreement?"

She nodded.

Max said laconically, "I hope, Mr. Mawr, you have some way of policing your gentlemen."

Edgar watched the game.

Max and Lucian, without the possibility of gaining new properties, would, as Chester had predicted, be starved out, though Lucian, with two monopolies, was still in a strong position. It seemed to Edgar that Max enjoyed his isolation. Was there not in him a residual Jewishness that would rejoice in every attack as a proof of prejudice? Yet, Chester had only acted naturally, combatting the tactics of Max with all his resources—and one of these resources was the group, the Wolgamuts. Edgar wanted to show Max that he was on his side, but there was nothing he could think of doing that would not appear ridiculously theatrical.

And Robinson. It was difficult for him to look at her; he was afraid she might return his look, dare him that way. She was doing well. Like Chester, she had arranged among the other players for a second monopoly. She was nervous and pale, excited by the game. Smiling every now and then, she would bite down on her lip as if trying to restrain her pleasure, or, as if it gave her the greater pleasure to gently bite down on pleasure. Her black hair was a rich background for her so pale face, and she was attractive to Edgar, more so than ever before.

She stood and invited Max to join her at the TRADERS' BAR.

Edgar went to stand by the window from where he would be able to hear their conversation. He lit his pipe and stared ahead as if he were just taking a break and not eavesdropping.

Robinson said, "I want my yellow, but I also want Chester's purple. I'll give you a fifteen percent concession on the yellow."

Max smiled.

Robinson looked down and said as if embarrassed, "You have no choice."

"Just so."

She did not understand.

"I go bankrupt with fifteen percent or without."

"You're angry with me."

He smiled.

"That I joined in with them. But I did so only to beat Chester. I'm sorry. I didn't realize I was hurting your game. Max, I'll give you a twenty-five percent concession."

"Why not forty?"

"But you're losing! You said so yourself. You don't have a chance to win. Why not let me?"

He smiled. He rubbed the back of his neck as if he had an ache. He turned to go.

Robinson called him back.

Edgar remained at the window, searching his own reflection there. Was it the conversation he had just heard or the reflection he faced that oppressed him? Forgetting it was still summer and hot outside, he wanted a breath of air, he wished he could open a window.

Donald was at his side.

"We were talking about a Luther."

"What about him?"

"Well," Donald said, "I wanted to know if you know him."

"Why?"

"I'm afraid I haven't the right to explain."

"Then I've never heard of him."

Donald, unable always to strike a hard bargain and willing to be seduced by others into trades of no advantage to himself, was the first bankrupt. Charles followed; he had expended himself early in the game in acquiring the smallest and most expensive monopoly, and then, by his agreement with Chester, had made his three pink properties valueless. Edgar was next. Max followed. Then Emily and Simon, both of whose games had been marked by prudence. None of the bankruptcies affected the game very much, for it was, even from before the time that Robinson had gained her yellow monopoly, a match between Robinson and Chester, Lucian a poor third. Each of the three had swallowed whole monopolies, but none could afford to rebuild more than a few houses on them.

The bankrupt players stayed about the board, some standing, some still seated on cushions.

Now Lucian was being eaten up, undergoing the experience of all the bankrupts, selling his houses for half their cost, then mortgaging his properties one by one until he had nothing left but debts.

Chester and Robinson continued, engaged in an almost equal contest, the winner to be determined by the fall of the dice. Chester threw them with a forced calm; Robinson dropped them close to her as if in order to be sure to be the first to see her luck. Chester was perspiring; he asked the bank for a loan. And though Victoria had formerly made her influence felt on the side of those participating with Chester in his agreement against Max and Lucian, she did not now have to consider even an instant before she refused. Robinson looked up with surprise, and Chester was hurt. Shortly thereafter, Chester was forced little by little to give ground until he finally stood from the board, managed a smile and said, looking at no one, as if a good sport in the face of many betrayals, "Vanquished."

6

Immediately as Edgar left Victoria's building, he felt the city heat. It was late, after eleven o'clock, and yet there were people everywhere on the park side of the avenue. Some had taken out folding chairs more comfortable than the hard wooden benches; there were even some baby carriages; but the other side of the avenue, the city side, was nearly deserted. The people faced the trees of the park, the river beyond. A group of students from Y lounged on and about a bench drinking canned beer. They started singing "Row, Row, Row Your Boat" and an aged couple at a neighboring bench seemed to join in with them, silently mouthing the words. One of the students nodded to Edgar apologetically, respectfully.

He had remained until the other guests had left, Victoria

at the piano, occasionally touching a key, pensively, the sound hovering for an instant, the maid noiselessly passing to and fro in the hall. Tired, he had wanted to speak of the evening, to catch at ideas, memories, that might explain this or that. Robinson. Robinson and Luther. He had felt unreasonably guilty, unmanly. And had waited for Victoria's attention, wondering then, her back to him, if she had troubled herself with even an instant's guilt that she had been so quick to accuse Max. He had stared at the nape of her neck and had felt cold even to his fingertips. And when she had turned to him, asking matter-of-factly, "It was Jane, wasn't it?" he had replied shortly, "Is that why you wouldn't help Chester to win? To strike at her conscience?" "Just so," she had replied, smiling at him, serving him with a mask.

Now Edgar felt the touch of a breeze on his brow. It pleased him to look at the people on the benches—small businessmen and their wives and families, workers who lived in the buildings behind those that faced the river. He thought of writing a poem; he would get in shape. How good to feel the ball full against the racket, and the backhand swing.

It would be a nice poem, a sad poem, a poem of community, and would lilt along like a song: people sitting together, their backs to the city, catching a breeze; someone might say hello to his neighbor, would use a cliché, but there would be sense and warmth to the cliché. The poem would be filled with banalities, so refreshingly banal.

He walked further south and now encountered fewer and fewer people. Perhaps it was the lateness of the hour and the people were returning to their apartments, to their beds. He thought of continuing his walk in the park but remembered that there were frequent muggings there. And his poem was then touched with a thrill of darkness, of stealth, and the people retreating to their apartments, and a walker walking among the shadows, anticipating a meaningless and yet just blow. He left the avenue to return by Broadway.

Here there was no breeze. The heat was infested with the fumes of automobiles and buses. The air wiped off on his handkerchief like grease. And every few minutes, a subway train passed beneath his feet, thundering, echoing. On the traffic island in the center of Broadway were some few benches; but the people here were Puerto Ricans, garish in their language, garish in the neon lights of hotels and store fronts. He could not like these people, could only disapprove of their colors, their strangeness, and he was afraid of being singled out by them, taller than them in their midst. He passed B's Cafeteria where one could pick up a whore, where, two years before, when he had had his "breakdown," he had sometimes gone when at four A.M. the bars had closed, had sat sipping his coffee, watching the whores make their marks. One night, he had watched a young hoodlum rifle the pockets of a sleeping drunk; when the old man was awakened by a too brusque movement, there, smiling across at him at his own table, was the hoodlum. The drunk accused him, and the hoodlum, in angry, violent terms, threatened the drunk, protested his innocence, horse-winked at the others in the cafeteria. The drunk searched for support in the faces of the whores and nighttime characters, but found none and, by the furtiveness, helplessness of his regard, had not expected to. Then, as before, he crossed his arms on the table and laid his head down on them.

Here, at the counter, a boy, perhaps seventeen years old, waiting to be served, had run a finger back and forth under his nose rubbing the space there red, his eyes watering. The waitress handed him his coffee and the boy then had the shakes, the cup clattering against saucer and spoon, violently, loudly, and the boy dropped it all and ran out of the cafeteria, dashed across Broadway, and then collapsed in a heap in a doorway on the other side of the street.

Two worlds. And one like himself could enter the second only if he observed the rules—stood by at a distance, a vicious witness to disorder and violence. Edgar no longer had a poem to write, no longer would phrase even a line, sure he would betray himself with his voice. That he would cry protest when he felt only fear and uncertainty.

He hailed a taxi and gave the driver Luther's address.

The room seemed larger in dim light. Smoke hung green, suspended beneath the ceiling, smelling sweetly. Luther was lying across his bed and the windowsill, his head bent back so that he could see up out of the apartment; he shifted his gaze down to regard Edgar, light from the street glazing his eyes. Robinson, barefoot in a black dress, walked to the bed and sat down on it not far from Luther. Then Edgar saw Max lying half-dressed on the mattress on the floor, his face glistening with sweat.

"How are you?" Edgar asked, starting towards Luther. But his friend did not move and Edgar stopped midway and then retreated to the armchair. His shirt stuck to his body; it was unbearably hot; his jacket would be creased out of all shape. He found himself looking uneasily from Luther to Max to Robinson's feet blackened by the city soot that thinly covered floor and chair and everything in the room.

Max said as if continuing an interrupted conversation:

"Your neck begins to get stiff, the muscles become tight, knotted, and then they begin to cut off the flow of blood, everything in your neck and back pressing against the arteries. Your pulse hammers wherever you touch yourself. You think if you'd only be able to mash your muscles soft, everything'd be all right. You want a hot, steaming bath, but at the same time, you've an aversion to water. The moment you think about it, your saliva dries and tastes awful. You want an icepack on your head because now the pain's general in neck and head and you're no longer sure where it started. No longer sure of anything. You're in a world outside of logic. And you can give in. You can start praying now, promise to build a cathedral if you're relieved. Or, you can hate. You can lie back and think that somebody did this to you, that the world's done this to you. You can hate everybody and everything. Delicious. You've got the proof in your head. And when it's over, you've a gentle craving for sugar. You know you deserve it, you deserve anything you want. Especially because the muscles remain tight, though looser, a reminder. They pluck at you after a while and say, 'Watch out, I'm still here, just waiting.'

"Migraines are worse," he continued. "My mother'd ask to be shot. Please shoot me, she said more than once. She probably liked the thought. Please shoot me. The drama of it. The finality of it. Please shoot me—as if, just a little, you've done so much, why not do that too? But what pain! Worse the migraines than cancer because with cancer they gave her dope. So then, knowing she was going to die, she changed her tune, more on key this time, and didn't ask to be shot—that was coming soon enough—but asked for more dope, begged for a shot.

"What I like, what I like most of all, is to be whipped, slapped. The first time it happened was a revelation, an ecstasy. She was a smart whore, a big-boned, blond, blue-eyed whore. She had only to look at me once to know what I really wanted. She made me lie flat on the bed, and then she straddled me, put her knees on my arms, and smiling at me, smiling, began to slap me hard, hard so that my cheeks stung. I didn't even want to protect myself. I'd never been so pleased. And then she consoled me, took me into her like a baby. It was, all in all, an act worthy of the Virgin. And it cost only ten dollars."

Luther had bent over Robinson; they kissed lightly, as if experimentally.

Max lay on his stomach, watching them, smiling unpleasantly, talking.

"Now everybody wants a captain. A big man. He's generous. He thinks big. He says, follow me and fulfil your destiny. Or, follow me and make money. Or, and this is the most insidious, follow me and the gates of heaven will open to you. It's a need, this captain, and there's no escaping it. But every time I decide to enlist, I think of the Virgin. There's my captain. She beats me and consoles me. It's a masque of man and god. It's beautiful, a ritual. Only, when you have two of you, both wise to it, why you can change roles at will: dispenser of punishment and consolation, and recipient of same. We should try it, Robinson. Luther? Luther's dead. He's dying the slow death. He won't last another year. But I will."

"But your headaches?" Robinson said, laughing.

"I'll give you part."

"There is no death," Luther said. "How can I die if there is no death?"

Max laughed.

Luther stood.

He asked, "I asked you, how can I die if there is no death?"

"That's right," Max said. "I hadn't thought of it that way."

"You're right I'm right. There is no death. Life is eternal and love is internal." He pointed rudely at Robinson's body and then sat down at her side.

"He looks so lonely," Robinson said of Edgar.

Luther was smoking; he looked indifferently at Edgar. Max said, "Robinson, give him a cigarette."

"I don't need one," Edgar said.

"You don't need one? I don't need one, Edgar honey, but you do. Why don't you just take one and let yourself go? Listen, I've got a game for you. I told your friend Charles about it and it delighted him. He thought it a 'grand' idea. It's a game I once thought of called: concentration camp. Half the people get undressed and crawl on the floor and the other half remain standing and just give orders. Anything that comes into their heads. I shouldn't laugh. It hurts me to laugh."

Edgar wanted to bring order to this room. But he wanted too to humble himself here.

"Go home, Edgar. Go home and marry the girl."

"I'll never marry," Robinson said, she alone laughing at her joke.

"You'll marry me," Max said. "A real wedding. With a hundred guests and champagne . . . Marry her, Edgar. You'll see it'll be for the best. You'll thank dear little Max for his advice one day. You'll see. You'll have a house in the country, and you'll have your little amusements, and one

day you'll be a department chairman. And a good one—
fair and decent and just . . ."

"You're wrong, Max," Edgar said. "You're wrong about
everything. You're bitter and you think I'm in the other
camp, you think I don't share your pain. But—you don't
know this—two years ago, I had a breakdown. Yes. And
I'd wake in the morning and couldn't face anything. That's
right. I couldn't face myself or my work. I'd wake and begin to wonder what I was doing here in my bed, here in my
classroom, here at my thesis. Even now. Only I've been
forgetting. I don't even recognize myself any more.

"I went back to bars—where we had been, the three of
us. I walked where we had walked. I went over every hope
we had ever had. And they were like nothing. Nothing.
They were just energy. And that energy was gone. Nothing took the place of nothing. Alex was right. Alex knew.
You can't help anyone, you can't do anything, unless you
go all the way, unless you love. And none of us really
knew how and none of us knows how. That's where we've
failed. We spoke of this and that, but all the time we were
just full of ourselves."

"A committee meeting on reform?" Max said. "With
eight pair of arms and nine heads and thirty-six hands, what
can't we accomplish? Love? My friend, I have pain. And
whom are you going to help? Why not help me? I want to
sleep with snow-white over there. The very least you can
do is arrange that she come here and rub my neck. A little
fix for little Max."

Edgar was shaking his head. Everything in this room was
too unclear, too hazy. He did not know how he could
make himself understood. He said, "There's nothing to
hang on to . . ." And even as he said that, Robinson was in
a pose, standing tiptoe on one leg and the other bent and

raised, the knee way up, her head thrown back, her black hair loose, falling free; and smiling then, teeth gleaming, twirling an imaginary baton, she began to strut like a drum majorette about the room. Luther reached for her as she passed him. She struggled in his arms, crying, "No, Mister Dirty, I don't want any of you." But then pressed herself to him, standing on the tips of her toes.

"She's wrong," Max said ruefully. "So wrong," he repeated ironically. "Edgar honey, please rub my neck."

Edgar found it impossible to look at Robinson and Luther and impossible not to.

"Edgar," Max insisted.

He sank weakly to his knees at Max's side.

It was awkward to massage him from here, and he did not want to go closer. How tight the muscles were. He began to knead the flesh of his neck and back, pushing it this way and that. He perspired heavily. He felt his hands powerful on Max's back and he pushed harder and harder until Max began to sigh. He looked up then. Luther had raised Robinson's dress over her thighs; he was kneeling before her. Edgar's hands were suddenly still and heavy as stone.

"No," Luther said, "this is no sweet virgin."

"You shouldn't do that," Edgar said.

Luther smiled at his friend for the first time and asked, "You want in too?"

Robinson rubbed one leg against the other; she bowed her head coyly.

"You shouldn't do that," Edgar repeated, standing, his eyes burning.

He stepped forward and then was kissing Robinson, clasping her to him.

"Go on!" Max cried, lying half off his mattress to see better.

Luther pushed Edgar roughly from Robinson.

Edgar heard Max's and Robinson's laughter even as he hurried down the stairs.

PART TWO
THE GAME OF DOSTOEVSKY

7

That night, Edgar dreamed he was in a very large piazza.
At one side was an arcade crowded with small, swarthy
men who, it seemed, were discussing business or sports,
something to do with numbers. However, the buildings
that gave on to the piazza were stately, and sculptures that
were well worth study were situated here and there about
the piazza.

It was a cobblestoned place and though that too added to
its charm, walking there was another matter; had Edgar
not been wearing sneakers, he would surely have slipped
and twisted his ankle.

He felt very young, very much a tourist, and there was a
spring to his every step. He left the piazza, entering a narrow street that, he realized after a moment, twisted and

turned so much, crossed so many other streets exactly like it, that were he to try and return to the piazza, he would have difficulty, and perhaps he was already lost.

At a street corner, he passed a group of smoking, silent, brooding young boys. For no reason, Edgar began to feel uneasy, and looking over his shoulder saw that the boys were following him—there were perhaps five. The street was deserted except for him and the boys; and each time Edgar looked back, there seemed to be more of them, and their faces, Edgar saw, were ugly, twisted, so that he suspected they were not children at all. He was again glad to be wearing sneakers, and he began to run, sure that he could, were it to come to that, outdistance the fastest of the short-legged urchins. But the next time he looked over his shoulder, the urchins were almost at his heels. He was very afraid. He ran as fast as he could and was breathless.

During the day, Edgar remained in bed, weak and headachy. He would not think and forced himself to look at things. The walls of his room had little to hold his gaze for long. But now they changed shape, formed a triangle, he at its base, and when he looked down at his feet, they were very small, as if he were twenty feet long. It was all a trick of vision. For, if he opened his eyes wide, everything returned to proper perspective.

Several times during the day, the phone rang. But Edgar would not answer. Victoria had probably called; the university surely would not hear of his absence at all, the students unwilling to so easily give up a good thing.

In the evening, he went to the kitchen to prepare himself something to eat. There it was already dark. He took but a glass of milk and some cupcakes back to his bedroom. The light was failing here too. He switched on a lamp and *though that satisfied him for a moment, he then began to wonder whether the apartment door were locked. He was sure it was; nevertheless, he went to check. It was locked and double-locked as it always was. He smiled at himself; he went to all the windows to see if they were secured. He felt the little locks—dusty; he thought that he would have to have someone come in soon to give the apartment a really thorough cleaning. He wished Victoria would send him her maid. . . . He stared at the window in his study that opened on to the fire-escape. The window was secured, but it would not be difficult to force it open. He breathed in deeply as if he were truly calm. He returned to his bed, brought his milk to his lips and suddenly sat absolutely still. He had heard a tapping in a nearby room. It stopped and started. He had difficulty breathing. Surely the noise came from another apartment. Again, he raised the milk to his lips; again his hands and body froze.*

He returned to the kitchen to find a weapon. Then he went to the study, kitchen knife in hand. He thought it would be best to turn off all the lights, to let the intruder think no one was up. In the bedroom, he thought he heard a noise in the kitchen. He half-turned, dropping into a crouch. "Who's there?" he demanded. He thought he had a fever he was so hot and cold. He sat in the dark in his big leather wingback chair, his hand on the handle of his knife, his eyes on the window.

Late in the night, he saw something pass across the window. He pressed himself back against his chair to keep himself from view. It did not pass again. But he was ready for it.

1

Victoria Harm thought she knew Edgar very well: he tended to be a dilettante, he was not industrious. But sometimes, she saw in his face the open and warm look of a very young man, the kind of decent young man it would have been right for her to have married five, six, or seven years earlier. And if she blamed him for his waste of years, she blamed herself for her own. Sometimes, she saw in him the makings of the kind of man she would be forty and fifty years old with. And if most of the time she saw in him someone to be mocked, she only disliked herself the more. It was, in any event, understood that they would marry upon Edgar's successful completion of his doctoral dissertation. Victoria regarded the completion of his thesis as a trial, a discipline that would continue throughout Edgar's new life. He would merit the promotions that would come his way; he would merit her respect. At least, she hoped things would work out that way.

When Victoria was eleven years old, her parents died in an accident and she was sent to schools first in New England, then in Switzerland, in Florence. By the time she was seventeen, she had begun to have affairs—nasty ones with young men not of her class. The psychiatrists, whom Victoria began to see shortly after her return to the States to attend college, informed her that there was in her a conflict between her moral sense and her wilfulness, between her desire for order and her scorn for it. They traced these conflicts to various roots—all equally plausible. But though Victoria, at the time of our story, was still with a psychiatrist—her "dentist" whom she saw once a week for an hour—she was hardly cured. For one thing, she feared death and none of her psychiatrists could do anything about that. Every month, when she had her period, she kept to her bed and would not see anyone. She had terrible cramps that made her feel old and ugly. And locked away, her thoughts went to death, to bottomless falling, to that nothingness. The best any of her psychiatrists could do was say that once married, the cramps might disappear.

Other than her psychiatrist, not even Chester Mawr, Victoria's dearest friend, had more than an inkling of her fear, her treatment, her many secrets. She had met the round man in Italy, both guests of a mutual acquaintance in a villa in Fiesole. Together they had toured Tuscany, each already familiar with it, each having at least one village where he knew of a masterpiece that the other did not know of. Their intimacy had been cemented by little things: by Victoria's being with Chester when the round man, so formal, had allowed himself a formless straw hat;

by their shopping together; by their sharing breakfasts. And though Victoria might smile at Chester's eccentricities, his penguin-like shape, she valued him highly. Indeed, it was Chester who had arranged that she meet Edgar.

Once, not long before our story, she teased her desire to tell Chester all, suggesting that he accompany her to her home in Connecticut. "We'll leave Edgar waiting and drive up north on the Merritt, only an hour, and then onto country roads, narrow lanes all lined by trees, up a little incline and into the roadway and there's the house. You'll like it. You'll like the way nearly all the rooms are on different levels, so old, and the way the chairs all seem like they're going to fall apart, but yet are strong, strong enough, once you know their weaknesses, to hold you, to last another hundred years. We'll take a walk in the afternoon and then sit by the fire and you'll talk, and you'll be just Chester and talk about this and that."

"Ah, Vickie. Misguided girl," Chester replied. "You persist in thinking that I can be 'just Chester.' But there is no 'just Chester' beneath my surface and I am all surface, albeit considerable." He continued, smiling gently, affirming the rules of all their converse: "You and I have no need of 'confidences,' no need at all. I know who you are. You are my Victoria who tolerates me because—may I flatter myself?—you have perfect discretion."

Victoria was, as has been previously mentioned, twenty-five years old. Her eyes were grey and very large; her forehead was high, and she kept her fine and light brown hair swept back and up. She was not particularly tall, though she gave that impression. Many would say she was striking.

One day, not long after the first Wolgamut evening of the new semester, Victoria saw Max Wise near campus. It was a lovely day, the first of a string of brisk Autumn days. The sky was a clear, cool blue; high above the city, some flimsy clouds were blown by the wind; and even the city buildings were revived by the light. Max walked hurriedly, staring straight ahead, his black hair askew. Victoria smiled remembering Edgar's picture of him walking on Broadway, his hands clasped so seriously behind his back. She thought he was the kind of teacher who would enter his classroom even as he was now, as if in a grouch, who would, of a sudden, perhaps in the midst of pacing, every eye on him, affront his students with a dramatic question, a revelation.

Close to the building she lived in, she saw a group of people standing about a doorway. A car was pulled up in the middle of the street; a police car was pulled up at an angle to the curb. Among the people were two Negro domestics, a doorman, a man with a dog on a leash. One of the policemen was taking notes; the other was directing traffic about the car pulled up in the middle of the street. Probably, a pedestrian had been hit by the car. An ambulance would shortly appear and the pedestrian would be taken to a hospital and cared for. Passing, Victoria could not help searching in the group for a glimpse of the injured pedestrian. She saw a stout woman, perhaps fifty years old, sitting up on the sidewalk, shocked and blanched.

Sometimes, seeing it was a fine day, Victoria might think to drive to the country. She knew it was silly of her, childish to, on the spur of the moment, drive into the country, but she did it just the same. Dressed still for the city in suit, heels, her hair swept up negligently, she would have her car driven to the door and would drive north to Connecticut.

A silly car—a grey, five year old Chevrolet she called Peregrine Moth. Some little thing was always wrong with it, technical things that Victoria knew nothing about, but that she could rectify by pulling out the choke, by tapping on the dashboard. And once in motion, opened up on the highway at a comfortable fifty-five, it was just fine.

Her property was considerable: there were groves of pine and within, on the blanket of pine, in the tangy air, one could hide from the day; there were chestnut trees, elm and birch—a large gnarled chestnut seared by lightning. There was a small waterfall. She liked to sit by it, midway up by it on a flat rock ledge. The property extended on one side to a lake; there was a boathouse where there had always been mosquitos, clouds of gnats; at twilight, rowing back, the first bats had swept from trees low over the lake.

She rarely stayed overnight. When she thought of the house, she remembered winds outside, embers in the fireplace flaming up; being warm in the flickering light, looking out a window at stars clear and cold in the sky.

One day, Victoria saw Max Wise following Jane Robinson into a taxi. She assumed that he was having an affair with her. She remembered how she had smiled thinking of him, and for no reason, remembered too the injured pedestrian. She thought Max had an unpleasant grace.

At dinner, Victoria sat across a nicely set table from Chester Mawr and asked: "What do you think of Mr. Wise?"

Chester smiled in a certain way.

"He is," Victoria admitted, "rather pushy. Will he push his way all the way up?"

"All the way up? My dear Victoria, he will surely become a famous professor. And one day, crowning the achievement of a fifth book of criticism, he will be offered a course of his own devising. He will appropriate to himself Homer and Shakespeare, Dante and Cervantes. He will call the course: Studies in Greatness. His classroom will overflow; he will be pointed out on campus, a celebrity. He will, in short, be a most popular diversion from the more serious and disciplined studies of English Literature and even Electrical Engineering."

She went to meet Edgar for lunch at the Boston.

The restaurant was smoke-filled, crowded with noisy university people. Edgar was there with Max and they rose to greet her, interrupting their conversation, organizing their table so that Victoria would be seated center, her back to the wall, at Edgar's side, facing Max. He, short, dark, with a nervous manner he employed as a social tactic, listened to Edgar describe his new game, The Game of Dostoevsky, and now and then awarded Edgar a fleeting smile, now and then glanced elsewhere, at the entrance, at another table. Nor did Max show much attention to Victoria, offering her his profile, his raised chin, his abstracted manner, an occasional mocking regard.

Victoria praised Edgar's new game; Max offered criticisms. But Victoria was not sure she approved of the game, and Max, she thought, would enjoy it. She took a peculiar delight in this reversal of positions.

*   *   *

At the second Wolgamut evening of the new semester, the guests entering Victoria's apartment saw in the center of the hall a wooden board of the same shape and size as the Monopoly board of the previous Wolgamut evening. In one corner of the board, as with Monopoly, was a square marked GO; between it and the next corner—marked GRACE —were squares in which were lettered, in the following order, PRIDE, COVETOUSNESS, LUST, ANGER, GLUTTONY; the adjacent side had squares in which were lettered ENVY, SLOTH, PRIDE, COVETOUSNESS, etc. On the board were two GRACE corners, diagonally across from each other; and each of the seven sins appeared three times on the board. In the center of the board was written in very large letters: DOSTO-EVSKY. At a little distance from the board was a chair and a small table; on the table was a name plate which read: GRAND INQUISITOR. At a side of the name plate was a stopwatch and a small stack of cards called Grace Cards. The hall was arranged exactly as it had been for Monopoly; cushions were about the board; the bar was in a corner of the hall and was stocked, however, with vodka, tomato and orange juice.

All the Wolgamuts were present: Victoria, Robinson, Emily and Donald Marwel, Chester, Edgar, Lucian Whittier, Charles Rizzo and Simon Parr. Max Wise was also present.

The Wolgamuts stood here and there about the hall.

Edgar coughed for their attention and said: "Any number may play.

"Each player will be given two identical symbols, one to mark his place on the squares of the board, and the second to indicate how many turns he's made about the board. For example, the first time he reaches the GO corner, he will put his symbol under the D of Dostoevsky. The second time he reaches GO, he will move his symbol to the first o of Dostoevsky. And so on. The first player to move to the right of the Y of Dostoevsky will be the loser.

"Prior to the game, we must decide on playing within

the context of a book or play we're all familiar with. It would be best to decide on the book at the evening before the evening we are to use it as a context, announce it, as it were, as an assignment. Also, each of us will have to take a turn as a non-player; that is, have to assume for an evening another position I will shortly describe.

"Players will throw the dice to determine the playing order; highest number will go first. Now the game begins. The first player throws the dice and then moves his symbol to the indicated square. If he throws a seven, for example, he will have to confess to envy in the name of a character from the book or play we've previously decided on. The confession must last no more than a minute and will be judged by the non-player called The Grand Inquisitor. It would be preferable for The Grand Inquisitor to be particularly familiar with the book decided on. He will, in any event, judge the confession on the bases of exactitude, interest, duplication, and, in confessions of great imagination, on the basis of plausibility. For, assuming that the book-context for the evening is *A Passage to India*, the first person to land on ENVY might confess to that sin in the name of Miss Derek, and, of course, will try to make his confession as thorough as possible. But now another player lands on ENVY. If he wants to confess in the name of Miss Derek, he must find new aspects, new proofs of her envy. In the course of a game, there will be approximately twenty confessions to envy. Twenty confessions to every sin.

"Now, if The Grand Inquisitor deems a confession well done, he may award the player a Grace Card. A Grace Card may be held indefinitely though no player may have more than one at any time. And, it may be used whenever the player likes. For example, the possessor of a Grace Card having thrown the dice and landed on a sin he is unprepared to offer a confession for, may elect to return his Grace Card to The Grand Inquisitor. And upon doing so, will, without offering a confession, move his symbol *back* to the nearest Grace corner. Also, as you will see, if the player throws an eleven or twelve, he might prefer to move back to a Grace corner, regardless of the sin, rather than be forced to move so many squares ahead. There are but twenty-four squares on the boards.

"If, on the other hand, the confession is, in The Grand Inquisitor's judgment, especially bad, The Grand Inquisitor may penalize the player by making him throw the dice a second time. If the confession is absolutely worthless, The Grand Inquisitor may penalize the player by moving him from wherever he is on the board *forward* to the GO corner and then have him throw the dice a second time. And there is no appeal from The Grand Inquisitor's judgment."

The Wolgamuts reacted favorably to Edgar's new game. Some questions were asked. Edgar suggested that they play the game this evening to familiarize themselves with it and, for this time only, that they play without a context—one could confess to any sin of any character of any book or play. Also, Edgar thought it best that he act as The Grand Inquisitor.

The players sat down about the board and the game began.

The Grand Inquisitor timed each confession; at the end of a minute, he raised his hand and the next player threw the dice. He awarded Grace Cards and punishments as he saw fit, without explanation. Some of the players attempted to do even as Edgar had suggested they would have to do in a game played within a context—confess in the name of a character already brought up by another player. Chester, following Lucian's lead, confessed to a sin of Lafcadio. Lucian then confessed to each sin he landed on in Lafcadio's name. Landing on LUST, he confessed to masturbation. There was no proof and yet The Grand Inquisitor awarded him a Grace Card. Donald Marwel revealed a knowledge of Tolstoi; Charles confessed in the names of Henry James' continental scoundrels. Jane Robinson used the world of Dostoevsky, and Edgar made a mental note that Dostoevsky would not do as a context. English novels would be best, the kind of books in which the characters' sins are not explicit beyond a certain point and thus are open to inference.

The game moved very fast. Much literature was at the beck and call of those present. Pride brought Lear to mind; Lear brought in the world of Shakespeare. There were too many sinners there. Emily confessed to sins in the names of characters from Kafka; but her confessions were too vague to be amusing. Simon Parr eruditely selected characters from novels only he had read. Victoria confessed to the sins of evil characters in fairy tales; Max confessed to the sins of fairy tale heroes. Victoria glanced at Max and, taking up his challenge, confessed to the sin of a fairy tale hero. It amused her then to twist the stories of her childhood. Max's knowledge of fairy tales was limited; he soon gave them up to look at children in literature. He went to Dickens and Victoria followed him there. Unable to emulate Max in confessing to nastier sins, she confessed in the name of Oliver though really for Fagin. And The Grand Inquisitor greeted imagination with Grace Cards and too literal confessions without a word and sometimes with a punishment.

He stopped the game to suggest that each time a player confess, the player shift into a kneeling position. Some of the players did so. Lucian offered one of his confessions with an air of contrition; nearly all the players developed, in the course of the evening, confessional styles; they copied each other; they improved on each other and on themselves. At one point, in the midst of a particularly good confession, The Grand Inquisitor realized he was not timing the confession.

*   *   *

It was past midnight and Victoria was preparing for bed when the doorphone rang. She paused an instant in brushing her hair. Her maid, standing in the passageway outside her door, informed her that Mr. Wise was downstairs, that he had lost his keys. Victoria smiled fleetingly. She told her maid to tell the doorman to ask Mr. Wise to come up, looking at and through her maid who, taciturn, would communicate her message to the doorman who would allow Mr. Wise to pass into the building.

2

Several days later, Victoria phoned Jane Robinson—with whom she had for some time thought she should have a talk—and invited her to lunch.

Robinson arrived at Victoria's apartment promptly at one. A neatly and casually set table was at the big window in the hall. Robinson, in raincoat, a boy's button-down shirt, skirt and heels, stood by the window, awaiting her hostess; she gazed at the river far below, holding on to her black shoulder bag. And Victoria, coming from her bedroom, dressed for shopping in a tailored tweed suit, small gold earrings which she was just then adjusting, thought Jane's attitude that of a governess in a romantic novel: pale, intense, overwhelmingly alone.

"I'm so glad you could come. Really, we see each other

so seldom and sometimes I have the impression I hardly know you any more."

"Have I changed so much?" Robinson asked.

"You have such lovely hair," Victoria said and suggested they start lunch.

They sat across from each other, and Robinson, still in her raincoat, wrapped in it, asked, "Would you say I've changed for the better?"

"Jane," Victoria said, "have you ever thought you need help?"

Lucian Whittier arrived by chance as Robinson left.

"A protégée?" he asked after her departure.

"A case study," Victoria answered curtly, gathering up her purse, gloves and umbrella.

"Is she then?"

Victoria smiled in spite of herself and her mood.

She replied, "I should hope not."

"I'm not intruding?" Lucian inquired.

"I am going shopping."

"What a coincidence! So am I."

Carrying Victoria's little bags and boxes, trailing along at her elbow, Lucian discoursed on "sordid" clothes, showing how one could, in one's own choice of clothes, and absolutely should, approach the border of Seventh Avenue styles, the charm in the brinksmanship. His conversation was filled with nice usages of adjectives and was pleasant to the ear, was music—"sordid" no more than a note at the lower end of the scale. And he demanded little in return for his conversation—one ear attuned to his wave-length was enough. Victoria smiled at him occasionally and now and then, between purchases, thought of her luncheon. Robinson had, the instant after Victoria's question, started to smile but then quickly had looked down and timidly nodded her head. Yes, she needed help. Then, looking out the window as if ashamed to face Victoria, she had begun a confession. "I really don't want to hear," Victoria had said, wanting to give Robinson the benefit of the doubt, that perhaps she had not seen the beginning of a smile, that perhaps everything could be arranged as simply as she liked. "Please," Robinson had said. "Coffee now or later?" "Luther Halverson . . ." Robinson had said and had gone on to identify him as Edgar's friend, to describe how she had met him. "And Max Wise," she had listed. "And once, with Edgar . . ." She had turned then an instant towards Victoria and Victoria had wanted to meet her face hard with the palm of her hand, sure that if it were not all a pack of lies, this was a lie. Edgar had not, could not, was not that kind of person.

Now in a taxi winding north through Central Park, Lucian commenting on the dreadful city skyline, on views of the city from above and below, on the wonderful view from her hall of the bridge, the river, the traffic below— exhilarated, ravished by that view—Victoria heard in Lucian's tone deeper notes, more operatic one might say. He said that the perspective from her window was the sole justification for tall, dreadful buildings. Victoria looked at him quizzically, smiling vaguely. Sufficient encouragement for Lucian to dare more. He spoke of Edgar's brilliance in devising entertainments, his tone hovering at the border of irony. She was sure that if she turned hot, he would too; if cold, he would turn cold, he attendant to her mood, to the liberties she might allow him. She said, "Dincha know, I call Edgar Mister Edgewater. He stands by the seaside, looking in, watching people doing things . . ."

"I would have said," Lucian said, "that he's really Mister

Master Of Ceremonies, the inventor and metronome of all our entertainments."

"Metronome?" Victoria asked, smiling.

"Tic, tac. Tic, tac," Lucian uttered, swaying regularly in spite of the motion of the taxi, smiling condescendingly then in a near perfect imitation of Edgar's smile.

Victoria dropped gaily into Edgar's wingback chair, letting umbrella and some small packages—a shower cap for Jane Robinson, some pairs of gloves for herself, handkerchiefs for Edgar, and a tie she wondered if she would give to Max or Edgar—fall to the floor. Lucian set his more heavy portion of her packages down negligently among open books and manuscripts on Edgar's desk and said, turning to Edgar who, taller than him by several inches, stood smiling host-like in the center of the room, "What a charming place!" He traveled then about the room, gracefully as if on wheels, remarking in passing how promising the drawings were. Fondling the antique frame of a miniature, he inquired whether it were genuine and frowned theatrically, applauded by a small smile from Victoria, when Edgar humorlessly replied in the affirmative.

"Tea?" Edgar inquired.

"Please," Victoria replied.

Lucian said that he would prefer something a bit stronger.

Edgar smiled condescendingly at Lucian.

Lucian laughed.

"What's funny?" Edgar asked, smiling still.

"Nothing, nothing. I was just thinking of a metronome."

Victoria smiled, and throughout their short visit encouraged Lucian in mocking Edgar.

*   *   *

When, as sometimes happened, Victoria met Max Wise on the street, she in the company of this one or that, they probed each other for weaknesses. The first time it happened, she with Chester, she searched Max's face even as he did hers, looking for some telltale mark, some surprise at the other's politeness. But there was nothing; they seemed equal in this game. "And where have you been keeping yourself, Mr. Wise?" Victoria asked, in her tone one meaning for Chester and another for Max.

Their more private encounters were just as cool, professional one might say. They hardly had need of secrecy, they met so quickly. The scene of most of their encounters was the Gotham Hotel on Broadway, some streets south of the university.

Now it should be understood that the university area was not entirely respectable. To be sure, there were, besides the university buildings which enclosed their green and tranquil quadrangle, many apartment buildings with double doors, always locked. And surely, all the buildings that faced the river were highly respectable. But Puerto Ricans and Negroes had drifted into the area between the river and Broadway, and they teemed in all the area east of Broadway. There, police always worked in pairs. Indeed, the university area was such that when, shortly after the second Wolgamut evening of the semester, tall, cave-chested Simon Parr was attacked by hoodlums in his very apartment, no one thought twice of it—such attacks were common enough for a person to think that it could happen to anyone but himself.

Perhaps the most sordid aspect of the university area was the so-called residence hotels. Once they had been apartment buildings, some even expensive ones with six-room apartments and maid's room behind the kitchen. But times had changed and nowadays they provided single rooms—some of decent size, some closet-sized—all furnished cheaply, gaudily; furnishings and walls soiled by the quick generations of occupants. Rents were payable in advance for the day or week and there were no monthly rates. These hotels infested the area—in ten square blocks there were thirty or so of them—and they were inhabited by blacks and whites alike. There were prostitutes, hoodlums; old people on their last legs and students making Bohemia of all this. They shared kitchens and bathrooms and one day missing a spoonful of jelly from the refrigerator and another day a morsel from an open tin of sardines, there were some who suspected each other, who peered out along the edge of their doors into the somber passageways each time they heard someone passing.

The Gotham, one of the largest of the residence hotels in the area, was a twelve story, box-like building. It faced Broadway; its entrance, however, was on a side street. The large lobby with marble pillars and marble benches was otherwise bare, as if the owner or owners of the hotel feared that anything moveable would, in fact, be moved. There were often clusters of men in the lobby—wizened and wise, standing in shadows, waiting for night. The elevator smelled of antiseptic cleaner. But the most disagreeable aspect of this hotel was its passageways. They were ill-lit; in certain of them, no matter what floor you were on, you had the impression you were underground—dank, grimy, oppressive places. The doors to the rooms were marked with letters and numbers, but whereas room 7B might follow room 7A, room 7C might be in another passageway, one of three branching off from where you stood. In this labyrinth, passageways divided here, swept off on a diagonal there; suddenly, you might meet one that transected the one you were in at an abrupt angle and that seemed to have no end but shadows. Footsteps resounded from afar; in the dim light, a silhouette brushed by you. All about were little, unidentifiable noises.

When Victoria once asked Max why he chose to live in the Gotham, he said that he liked the smell. Victoria thought otherwise. She thought that he liked this room doubly that it was a convenient but dirty place to meet her in. She came to him, through the passageways, umbrella in hand.

3

Luther Halverson liked to drive at night, to leave the city on any one of the complex of highways that fed into it. Then, further and further from the city, the highway becoming deserted, lit only by the headlights of his car, he became most alert, most alive. More and more, he drove with Robinson. They had no destination and nothing but time, the lassitude of sunrise, to stop their course. They went at high speeds, racing against their own headlights, the night wind cold, burning against their skin. Some mornings, they found themselves in places like Harrisburg, Pennsylvania, in Portland, Maine. They would sleep there the day. Several times they were away from the city three, four days. On the road. Going no place. Silent and at night.

Once, high on marijuana, Luther mocked himself, saying

to Robinson that he would get some money and they would go to Mexico. They would each, he said laughing, write wordless books, paint pictures with their eyes closed. They would disappear south with no thought of return and there, in Mexico, in perfect silence, in the perfect solitude of night, would sit side by side and contemplate each other, every muscle and nerve of each other, identify liver, pancreas and heart without words, be each cell of each body so that life would have a unity with god.

Max Wise was too often with them. He would stay in his corner of the room, laughing nearly silently if they talked in his presence, and when Luther would look at him, Max would be looking at a book, as if he had been laughing at something there. One night, when Luther was high, Max approached him and said, "What's new in Tibet, O holy father?" Robinson, whom smoking never affected as it did Luther, laughed at Max's joke. And Luther, on top of the world, felt something gnawing at his peace. He said, "Get thee hence, Satan!" So that Robinson and Max both laughed the harder.

One night when Luther was alone in the apartment, Edgar dropped by.

Luther imagined he was here to redeem his pride, to, embarrassed at what had happened the last time he had been here, show that it meant nothing to him. Luther could not care less whether Edgar had been embarrassed or not, and he would have indicated as much except that Edgar had such a prosperous look about him. He wore a dark suit, a black, rakish hat, and if he seemed pale, Luther only marked that up to the dim light of the room.

Luther sat on his bed.

Edgar sat in the armchair and asked whether Max did not, now and then, get in his way.

Luther did not bother to answer.

Edgar smiled condescendingly.

He asked: "Have you ever thought that there's but one normal state—paranoia? Have you ever thought, in short, that you have every reason to be afraid of your own shadow?" He laughed. He said, as if parenthetically, "No, not Luther. You're too healthy for that.

"The sensation is strange. It comes only at night. You are sure that someone is looking over your shoulder. Of course, he's out to get you. But, he takes his time. And you begin to wonder whether it wouldn't be better if he were to really make his play. And then you begin to wonder whether that is his very game, that, no matter what you do, he will always be at your shoulder . . ."

He continued in such a way, making rhetoric of his fears.

During one of his more pensive pauses, Luther asked him if he would lend him a hundred dollars.

Edgar was a bit taken aback. But he smiled and said, "I like you, Luther. At the very least, you're frank. Direct. You always were. But do you really mean 'lend'? And, as I think about it, why not ask Max? Or Robinson? She's got money, you know."

"Will you or won't you?"

Edgar acknowledged that he could afford fifty dollars.

When Luther next saw Robinson, he asked her to lend him five hundred dollars.

She blanched. She said she did not have that much money.

He could see she was lying.

She said matter-of-factly, "But whatever gave you the idea I had so much money?"

He said nothing. He would not think about it.

Luther put on a suit and tie and went to his publishing house, looking for an advance on a new novel. It was to be a Western, something he had long considered. But, wanting to outline it to his editor, he found that it was, as of now, impossible of verbalization. He improvised an outline. He could see the editor fidgeting. It angered him; it amused him. He went on, growing more and more voluble, until the editor, unable to restrain himself, reminded Luther that regardless of the story, he owed the publishing house money for a previous advance, that he had not published anything in more than a year and that he would be very happy to see the manuscript of the Western when it was finished.

He made the rounds of the paperback houses; there was nothing to be had from them. The humiliation of presenting himself in suit, in conciliatory manner, and then being turned down was lessened however, by the knowledge that they were not refusing his book, but only the story he recounted to them (and each time, he altered it a bit, gave it flourishes); and, they were not refusing him—he who they saw was but an actor, an emissary of the real him. All the more reason that when returning to his apartment from one of these futile midtown expeditions, Robinson saw him for the first time dressed in suit and tie, and began to laugh, and said that he looked, except for the lack of a hat, like one of those east-side peddlers, he laughed with her, thinking it was not really a joke on him. And when she insisted that in honor of his wearing a suit, he take her out to dinner, the first time he would ever have "gone out" with her, he agreed, not even bothering to see if he had funds. Which, when the dinner was over, he discovered he had not. Robinson was not amused at that. She extracted the necessary money bill by crumpled bill from her cavernous purse and handed them to him publicly.

*   *   *

One night, returning home from a solitary drive, elated, exhausted, Luther entered his apartment and found, placed prominently on his bed, Robinson's journal. The journal was bound and was of book size. It was not easy to read, above all in the state Luther was in. Sometimes, the print was small, precious; sometimes, the writing was scrawled in hastily, unevenly. The last entry was written in a form not previously used in the journal and was as follows:

Eveline stood in the lobby of the DeWitt hotel, clearly, by her indecisive air, there for some illicit purpose. She was a tall, slender girl—no more than seventeen years old; her eyes were large, black, innocent; her hair fell free, was long, black, the kind of hair that until yesterday was in braids, but that now hangs free, disorderly. She wore a dirty white raincoat which she hugged to herself nervously, as if for comfort, such a thin comfort. All about her were high ceilings, pillars, potted palm trees, soft chairs and sofas, and everywhere, seated or standing in groups, were cigar-smoking conventionaires—tall, fat, short, with little tags in their lapels: Mike Haskins, Talahassee, Fla. Surely, there is something sensual about innocence, for though the host of men standing about might have thought that this girl, so forlorn in their midst, so hesitant, was someone's child—her father, when he came to New York, stopped at the DeWitt, her father a nice man

who had, when her cat had been run over by a car,
bought her another without delay—they looked at her
knowingly, finding her—so young for this—especially sin-
ful, and some stared at her, wetting their lips with reproach. And does not action bring about reaction? So that
Eveline, so timid, nervous, smiled smally, unevenly, a
twisted smile.

She finally presented herself at the desk. She said she
was Mrs. Reventlow, has my husband arrived? A clerk
phoned to room 962, to the Russian who, for the night,
at Eveline's insistence, went by the name of Mr. James
Cunningham Reventlow, cotton broker from St. Louis,
Mo. Did he, so dark under so light a name, enjoy the joke
on him, the condition she had imposed on him even as
she had imposed conditions on herself, for humiliation,
for spite? Who had been waiting no less than an hour
and a half for the now soon to come dénouement. Impatiently, she hoped. Nervously, she hoped.

The young bride, without even a ring or a piece of
baggage, just a big black Italian shoulder bag, followed
the bellboy—submissively, head hanging, smiling in her
twisted way to herself all the way, in the elevator, down
the corridor, smiled that way as she entered the room.

He, handing the bellboy a tip, peeling it off a roll of
bills—no secret between him and the bellboy that he was
no Reventlow—was all dark-eyed intelligence and flabby
flesh. All open animosity as if what he wanted was to hurt,
to prove himself right that there is no tenderness and
nothing good, but only being adept in a world so well
understood as rotten.

Did he, upon seeing her, resume in a so tender smile
not his impatience but his laughter during the time he had
waited—at her hesitations, at her horror of each step forward she had taken? Did he omit to mention her tardiness
because he saw written on her face, in her manner, that

she would bolt, that she, reminded of what she was doing here, would cry out? He closed the door and she was then in the den, so right a place for all that was sordid. The pastel-tinted room (was it not that that she had wanted?), the flowered bedspread, the flowered paintings, the whirring, buzzing sounds of the air-conditioning, the television set on wheels.

She sat down in an armchair, wrapped her raincoat about her as if preserving herself within some sort of cocoon, a cocoon of herself, of her youth. She sat there, miserable that she was betraying Luis—weak-willed, who had taken money from the Russian and let him mock him to his face. Rubbing the sore on his lip while the other laughed. The Russian had installed himself in the other's apartment as if he owned it and never a word of protest. Stayed in a corner of the room, giving it his very smell, so that sometimes, even when he was not there, she felt that he was, watching, waiting. For this. Eveline felt weak, alone and bitter enclosed in this room with a man twice her age. She wanted to cry, but instead, she looked at the dark man and said, "It's bad to betray a friend, isn't it?"

He nodded, smiling.

"I mean," she said, "it's bad to go to bed with your best friend's girl, isn't it?"

He laughed.

She too. Opened her lips, laughing in an innocent, sensual way.

When Luther had finished reading, he left his apartment and drove almost as far as Maryland. But early in the morning, he called on Robinson at her dormitory. She was sleepy-eyed when she came downstairs, timorous, almost sarcastic.

He took her arm.

She went unwillingly, had, like a child, to be almost pulled to the car.

They drove off. Luther drove all through the day, south again, this time behind trucks, in heavy traffic, so that driving was not pleasant at all, but slow, tedious. At one point, he pulled off the road to rest. When he awoke, it was night, and Robinson was at the wheel and they were arriving in New York.

4

Victoria saw more and more of Lucian Whittier, having the Fine Arts Instructor accompany her to the theater, a concert, or *tête à tête*, at lunch, dinner. They liked the same music—Mozart, Haydn, music full of variety and clear sounds. Yet, listening once to a Brahms symphony, Lucian seemed delighted by that as well. When Victoria commented disparagingly on the music, Lucian evoked an image of the full-bearded composer sitting stiffly at his piano discovering a theme, playing it this way and that, in a Mozartean way, and then in a national anthem way, and Lucian smacked his lips at the latter, saying emphatically as if he were the composer and the composer were a silly old man, "Now that is the way music should be written." It seemed to Victoria that Lucian could find delight in almost anything—that all things were equal to him and nothing was overly dwelled on. He could develop a position in defense of the most indefensible thing and be, if not convincing, charmingly outrageous. And, in regard to Victoria, he evinced a perfect understanding and a nice discretion, making Victoria feel that in his company she was seconded in all things.

Walking together on campus one day, Victoria and Lucian met Max Wise who, hurrying from one class to another, stopped an instant to talk, to look, perhaps to enjoy the ambiguities of all his public conversation with Victoria. He was wearing, Victoria noticed, the red and white striped tie she had bought one day when shopping with Lucian—'a peppermint tie,' Lucian had called it—and though Victoria was sure that if anyone could put two and two together it was Lucian, she was not afraid of his inevitable discovery. She might have preferred it otherwise, but, the case being what it was, she said at the first opportunity, standing taller than the two men—Lucian speaking of the Game of Dostoevsky, of *The Tragic Muse* which he was reading and would re-read for the next Wolgamut evening—"My, what a lovely tie." Max addressed Victoria a mistrustful glance as if he were afraid more than anything of being mocked, or, Victoria wondered in that instant, as if he might, of all things, be jealous of Lucian. Lucian said that the tie was indeed exquisite, but, he warned, very demanding. He said a tie like that should be worn on a pale blue shirt with yes, a somber suit, but very well pressed; and perhaps a hat like he had recently seen Edgar wearing, rakish, though less sinister.

"The tie," Max said, "is a gift from my mother."

"Oh really?" Lucian said.

"Really."

"Then your mother's taste, wouldn't you say, runs to the rakish?" Lucian said.

With Lucian, she met Edgar one day for coffee at the Boston.

Seated, chin raised, hair swept back, she said to Edgar: "Everyone has only praise for your game. I, however, begin to think it somewhat risky. Don't you think some of us might be tempted to make unfortunate confessions?"

"Yes, I do," Edgar replied with a smile.

Lucian said, "Unfortunate only for those who have something to hide. As for myself, I do, therefore I am. I am, therefore, I tell. I tell, therefore I am amused."

"But," Victoria said, smiling at Lucian, the patron of his wit, "there's so much to tell and so little worth telling."

"That," Lucian said, "is the problem of the masses. But, for some others, what's most distressing is that we have so very much worth telling and so few opportunities to do so."

Edgar smiled patiently. He said, "Robinson has solved that problem. She's thinking of going to an analyst."

"Hardly a solution," Lucian said. "That's neither amusing or absolving. It's most tediously only reconciling."

Victoria wondered quickly how much Edgar knew, how much Jane Robinson had told him—where? doing what? She said coolly: "Did Jane tell you of this project in all intimacy?"

"Just so," Edgar replied condescendingly.

"I did not know," Lucian said, "that you knew the girl so well."

"Who should say I do not?"

"Indeed, I would not," Victoria said.

"Oh," Edgar said carelessly, "I see her now and then."

"Now and then?" Lucian said. "Do you see her now and then as a tutor? For example, as a tutor of poetry, exercising on her a second influence, a welcome one surely after the how shall I put it, sedentary influence of our friend, Donald Marwel?"

"I am not," Edgar said, "a poet. I have not the necessary imagination."

"Ah, revelations!"

"Intimations," Victoria corrected.

"From a bankrupt," Edgar said smiling.

"A bankrupt?" Victoria repeated.

Then she asked, "Is it you who suggested she undertake analysis?"

Their looks crossed and Edgar seemed faintly amused, reluctant to reply. He said, "I too do not approve of analysis."

"Nor of those who do?" Victoria asked.

"That's something else again," he replied.

*　　*　　*

Max Wise, Victoria discovered, had at least a second sore spot.

One day, in his room in the Gotham, she asked him what it was to be a Jew. "Is it," she asked politely, "a religion? a race? a people?"

Smiling caustically, he said it was an intellectual position.

"How so?"

"You say no to everything. On principle. We take our roots from Judas."

"You think," she said smiling, "that I don't like Jews?"
"I never would have said so."

"Is it part of your Judas principle to betray?"
"Exactly."
"Then aren't you really a sentimental?"
"Why?" he asked, amused.
"That you can think in such terms."

"Tell me about your parents."
"What would you like to hear?"
She disliked his tone. She felt that in spite of their differences, or perhaps because of them, she had a certain sympathy for him.
"My mother," he said, "tried to commit suicide."
Victoria was surprised. She would have pictured his mother as kind, generous, florid. "Why?" she asked, wondering just the same if he were lying.
"She had cancer. And she knew it. So, insufficiently drugged, she climbed on her hands and knees up four flights of stairs to jump. But, she was discovered." Victoria had turned from him, was adjusting an earring. "On the other hand," he said, speaking slowly, with evident relish, "my father never tried that. But, when he was dying, he was, for one reason or another, always spitting. He had a little spitting cup. And when he had visitors, he'd be looking full at them, gathering up his phlegm, and he'd enjoy the polite fear people had that he'd spit at them."

"Don't you think," Victoria asked, "that there are two teams? The blues and the others?"
"The others?"
"The grubby ones."

"The blues then?"
"You know, don't you?"
"People, you mean, with a taste for the grubby?"
"Just so."

It rarely happened that Victoria slept with Max. Yet, once or twice, she did fall asleep at his side. And once when that happened, she awoke but did not move, not even to open her eyes, feeling his lips on her body. Surely, it was dark in the room, she in repose, her body long, slender; he leaning over her, his every touch touched with a terribly distant tenderness. It bordered on a dream.

One day when she was with him in his room, the announcing pains came.
She took a pill from her purse.
He saw her and smiled sarcastically.
He knew nothing of her. She took, in fact, other precautions, first-rate precautions, but that, she thought, counted almost for nothing. She was convinced she would never give life.

At home, she phoned Lucian to inform him that she had a headache and could not make dinner. She enjoyed the doubt on the other end of the line. She thought that with nearly all the people she knew, headaches, pains, were tactics, things invented behind which one played for position. Her pain, her two or three days of pain were all her own. She was on her bed, bent almost double, her head by her knees, because even drugged she had cramps, pains like tightening cords inside her belly.

The following day, her pain was constant but distant, as if her mind were removed from and untouched by the pain, looking through a screen at it. Her body was a corrupt thing and was repugnant to her. She thought of Max leaning over her. She wanted to laugh. And then she smiled at this secret, that tomorrow or the next day she would again be Victoria.

The third day, even drugged, she suffered greatly. Her doctor had told her that she should not increase the amount of drugs she took, that were she to do that, she would, month after month, have to increase the dosage. The pain was unbearable. She reached out a hand and closed it as if on another in air. She thought of Max's mother, florid and kind, crawling four flights on her hands and knees—her inevitable tears at being discovered. She wanted to cry for mercy. Her maid would come. Her maid would hold her hand if she asked. In spite of her pain, she smiled at that picture.

8

Every night now, the nighttime fear visited Edgar. It was absolutely unreasonable, but knowing that did not help. It was. It was so real that he never thought of it as internal. It was not the nervous reactions of his body that came first, but the presence, external, faceless, somewhere about him. It was worse if he lay prone on his bed; his only defense was staying cool, aware, the lights on.

Some nights, waiting for dawn, he wandered Broadway and the side streets there just as Max Wise had, only he walked with a smile, forced at first, unnatural, and a black, rakish hat. He thought of buying a walking stick and told himself that that would be madness, that one had no right to give in so thoroughly to one's fancies. He felt watched, but he was a big man and he made himself walk with a measured step. He saw sights he had seen before, the ugly sights of drunks, of prostitutes, of police frisking Negroes, Puerto Ricans. And it was like a confirmation of he would not phrase what. Smile to it and walk with a measured step.

5

When the Wolgamuts gathered at Victoria Harm's apartment to play the Game of Dostoevsky a second time, certain of them had with them editions of Henry James' *The Tragic Muse*. This assiduity was surely a tribute no less to James than to Edgar. For if Edgar's game had, if only in expectation, already become a success with nearly all the Wolgamuts, *The Tragic Muse* seemed by its wit and tone, by its characteristic quality of saying much without saying all, a most excellent context for the game. Also, the dramatis personae of the novel were numerous and various: there was a promising politician turned painter; a diplomat enamored of the theater; an aristocratic young lady who would have made of the promising politician a prime minister had he not turned promising painter; there was an esthete, brilliant and witty; some French characters; a host of brothers, sisters, parents; and, there was the tragic muse herself, Miriam, an actress who, at the conclusion of the novel, was on the high-road to fame and perfection of her art.

The board on which the Wolgamuts would play was, as usual, in the center of the hall. There were nine cushions placed about it, and The Grand Inquisitor's table was at a little distance from the board, above it. It had not yet been decided who would be The Grand Inquisitor, and Edgar, wandering among the guests—everyone had arrived but Jane Robinson—inquired of this one and that if he or she would undertake that responsibility.

As usual preceding a Wolgamut game, the guests circulated much: little knots of two, three or four establishing themselves by the bar, the piano, splitting then, a new group formed by the big window, underneath the copy of "The Birth of Venus," people and reflections moving here and there.

Donald Marwel stood a moment with Max Wise.

The Russian scholar maintained that Henry James had a serious limitation, that he saw everything against the background of art and art was *a priori* judged supreme. He suggested, developing his thesis at some length, with many ironical smiles, that a psychological study of James would offer a better clue to his work than a close reading. He turned then to Donald's poetry; he said that all things considered, Donald was probably the best of the university poets.

Donald replied mildly.

He knew Max very well; he was like a dozen others. He was not a New Yorker by choice, but by birth. He thought and would always think that a living room, a classroom, wherever he was where there were others, was an arena. He did not talk and converse, he performed and competed. And he sadly abused himself in doing so even as he abused the object of his mockery or flattery.

Chester Mawr, who had seen very little of Victoria of late, stood with her and Lucian Whittier and, urbane as he was, could not hide from his tone certain nuances of reproach. But Victoria, sparklingly lucid—Lucian feeding her lines so that the conversation was really between Chester and Victoria—was so clever and arbitrary, as she could so charmingly be, that Chester, in the pleasure of the conversation, pardoned all.

About Simon Parr, who rarely attracted attention—his manner so drab and toneless—was a little group that soon grew in size. He wore his suit jacket over his shoulder; his right hand was in a plaster cast. He recounted what had happened to him. It was a Friday night and he was home reading. Someone rang the doorbell and said, "Western Union." Simon opened the door and before he could know what was happening, three Negroes pushed their way in and knocked him to the entrance way floor; the hoodlums, who otherwise did not show themselves very experienced, did close and lock the door. In a way, the initial beating—over the head and shoulders with blunt instruments—was fortunate, for Simon, during the next few minutes, was that stunned that he felt almost no pain, had no fear. He saw everything hazily. The hoodlums seemed to him red-eyed, ape-like, perhaps drunk or high on drugs. "They took my typewriter, my wallet; they left the apartment an absolute mess; they broke, unreasonably, most of my record collection; and when they were leaving, one of them, again without reason, stamped his foot down on my hand and then kicked me here and there. As I think about it now, it was incredible and quite lucky I didn't scream. They surely had knives or razors and might have panicked and done worse. In any event, my hand was broken. I crawled to the phone with great difficulty since, on my right side, I couldn't use my hand, only my elbow, like a crutch.

"At the hospital, the nurses were not terribly kind. I think, however, that was to be expected. They deal with such things all the time. They thought I was a drunk or a homosexual—because, you know, those people are frequently attacked. And since it was a Friday night, they were very rushed. That has to do with paychecks—there are more 'muggings' Friday nights than at any other time.

"There is little hope of catching the hoodlums. In fact, were I to see them again, I doubt I would recognize them— brutal, black faces. They, however, have nothing to rejoice over. My typewriter is worth to them, a detective told me, no more than a tenth of its real value. And the cash I had in my wallet came to no more than twenty-eight dollars."

Though, in general, one could listen to Simon with but half an ear—everything he said so neatly organized that if you followed him in the beginning, you lost nothing much if you lost him in the middle—this time, he was, in every detail, listened to with great interest, and when he was concluding his account, all the Wolgamuts present, even those not in the group immediately about him, were of his audience.

Charles Rizzo, lean in his severely cut dark suit, said that the hoodlums, when caught, should be flogged.

Simon said that he did not desire vengeance, that, in fact, he had very little feeling at all about the men who had attacked him.

Edgar was insisting a second time to Chester Mawr that he—perhaps of all the Wolgamuts the most familiar with the work of Henry James—act as The Grand Inquisitor when Jane Robinson, accompanied by Luther Halverson, arrived. She had, one could see, recently been to the hairdresser. She wore a black sheath dress; her lips were faintly rouged; and she carried herself, on heels, with a certain theatrical grace. And, of course, Luther Halverson, a newcomer, attracted interest. His beard was neatly trimmed; his suit, however, was old, double-breasted, out of style. His smile and manner were positively fatuous; and his eyes were bright, full of an inner knowledge. Some of the Wolgamuts knew him; some knew of him; others might have said they had suspected his existence. In any event, he was introduced by Edgar and he provoked some smiles. Max needed no introduction and he kept his distance, bowing politely. Luther bowed in turn, loosely, his body all elastic, he surely seeing Max first here, then there. Attracted to the window, the reflections there, dim New Jersey, looking that way, smiling in his way, as Edgar led him about the hall like a country cousin.

To Victoria, Edgar risked that Luther was his first barroom companion; to Chester, he said that Luther was his former student. Which information prompted Chester, a moment later, to say ruefully to Victoria that he was beginning to wonder whether it was, after all, worthwhile to be a teacher.

Robinson said that Luther was prepared to play with them this evening.

*   *   *

Early in the game, it became clear to Chester, The Grand Inquisitor, that many of the Wolgamuts in reading *The Tragic Muse* and considering it as a context for the Game of Dostoevsky, had found among the many characters there, one who was more or less congenial to themselves, or, to their purposes. Emily Marwel—for whom Chester could not at all find a counterpart in *The Tragic Muse*—had identified herself with the aristocratic Julia; Victoria—who might have identified herself with Julia— did, like Miss Robinson, identify herself with the actress, Miriam; Charles Rizzo, Max and Edgar had all identified themselves with the esthete, Gabriel Nash; and Lucian Whittier—who, Chester thought, might have best fit the role of the esthete—took for himself the role of the politician-turned-artist, Nick Dormer. At the beginning of the game, only Donald Marwel and Simon Parr confessed in the names of various characters—their confessions the most literal of all. Luther Halverson confessed to sins of a secondary character, the unpromising actor, Basil Dashwood.

Chester, seated above the game, found all of this confusing, if, for a time, entertaining. The three Gabriel Nashes, for example, had little in common. Charles Rizzo's Gabriel Nash was the pure esthete, removing himself in the course of Charles' confessions even from the context of *The Tragic Muse;* Max Wise's esthete was more dark than fair, standing at a side of *The Tragic Muse* and mocking the characters therein; and Edgar's Nash was no doubt his version of Lucian Whittier, a nice attack. In short, confessions were, if derived from the context, rarely confined to it; they were dialogues with special meanings for several players; and many confessions were answered, ramified, or annotated in following confessions.

Emily Marwel confessed in the name of Julia proudly, chin up, head held back, having taken it upon herself not only to be Julia, but to mimic Victoria. And, in spite of her efforts, her Julia seemed more and more to be about forty-five years old, and the impression she gave touching her dry red hair in a gesture she might have thought of as regal, was one of high nervousness. She spoke, she thought, in the manner of Julia-Victoria; it struck Chester's ears as a high-pitched impersonation of herself, less amusing than embarrassing. She had a rather limited if vaguely flattering understanding of Julia, making her too much the puritan to be really guilty of anything but pride. Happily, her confessions did not last too long, and happily, she was able, for a time, to base them on events of the novel.

Lucian, attacked by Edgar, returned the favor, making Nick Dormer into a dilettante who, taking himself too seriously, was comical. He had Nick wavering between politics and art as between two affectations, and he did not fail to characterize him as an "edgewater." All this, Lucian did in a perfect copy of Edgar's manner: a false regret and a most marked condescension. And yet, Lucian did not give a consistent picture of Nick Dormer; feeling himself obliged to answer Emily's Julia confessions, he sometimes made Nick into an honorable sort, estimably finding occasions for him to praise Julia.

Robinson created, little by little, a Miriam history of some originality: her father had been a man of affairs, rich, powerful; he had raised his daughter in hotel suites in all the great capitals of Europe; she had worn white; her hair had been long, combed out for her every morning and evening by a maid with a smile; everyone had smiled—purchased to do so though Miriam did not know that until years later. Sights had been kept from her. She had visited botanical gardens in this city and that, but did she not remember how, in her father's carriage, driving through a low neighborhood of Vienna, her English governess, for she had had several, had drawn the shades? But then her father had died, leaving her poor, without a *sou*.

As Robinson slowly, methodically, developed a history of Miriam, Victoria more impatiently had Miriam already embarked on her career. She spoke of Miriam's relations with Gabriel Nash, making Nash into her first protector, intimating as well that Nash was her *amant*. She cleverly gave to Nash certain qualities of Lucian Whittier and certain of Max Wise. And, not surprisingly, Lucian, as Nick Dormer, established that he was a particular friend of Gabriel Nash, and Gabriel Nash was, in spite of everything, not without charm.

If these confessions, the way certain of the players twisted out of shape the facts of *The Tragic Muse*, began to disturb Chester, that disturbance was nothing to what he felt listening to the over-long confessions of Luther Halverson.

Clearly, Luther had not read, or at least not recently, *The Tragic Muse*. Perhaps, Chester thought, he had "boned up" on one aspect of the book, or, he thought, then admiring Miss Robinson, been "boned-up." In any event, Luther understood Basil as, quite simply, a dog on a leash, an escort to Miriam. He was fed, housed, tolerated and pitied by her. He put himself in a *fiacre*, smiling at the sound of the word,

the air of verisimilitude it created, and for nearly two minutes had himself waiting for Miriam while she visited one
of her admirers—Chester could not tell which. Miriam had,
fortunately for the confession, left her purse in the *fiacre*,
and Basil, overly curious, opened it and went through her
correspondence there: a letter from Nick Dormer, another
from the "diplomatist," Sherringham, and one from "what
is his name, the poetaster?" Luther was voluble to an ex-
treme; he affected to speak in the way Henry James wrote,
but he lost the grammar if not the sense of his sentences
midway. With a fatuous smile, to the smiles of others, and
the close attention of two or three. Chester felt called upon
to remind him that confessions must last no more than a
minute. Later, he felt forced to issue penalties. And, as he
looked about the board, he estimated which of the players
was really concerned about the freedoms Luther and, in
fact, almost everyone else was taking. Not even Victoria.

* * *

Max Wise's Gabriel Nash was the nemesis, at least for a
time, of the diplomat and future ambassador, Sherringham.
He said that unknown to everyone else, he had taken Sherringham on a tour of Paris bordellos. He concluded that
Sherringham had not been affected by the experience at all.

Emily, at her next turn, said that she had indeed heard of
the bordello episode and that though she had not, from
sloth, wanted to believe it— "Oh, my dear Emily!" escaped
from Chester—she did now and that was the reason she
would not marry Sherringham. Chester reminded Emily
that, after all, Sherringham was Julia's brother.

But if Emily's attack on Sherringham seemed to Chester
to be, like Max's, an imprecise attack on some player at the

board, Donald nevertheless accepted it as a challenge. He confessed then in the name of Sherringham. He did so with good grace and he, more than any of the other players save Simon Parr, stuck to the events of the novel. He stressed the passionate quality of Sherringham, that way answering those whom he assumed had imposed this identity on him that there was little, if anything, in common between him and the diplomat. He confessed to desiring Miriam, making Sherringham appear a poor fellow, though well-bred, bitter in his profession of diplomat in spite of the fact that he, with only a little application, was bound to succeed.

Perhaps that confession had not been meant as an attack on Edgar. Nevertheless, during the confession, Victoria smiled in a particular way.

Max now chose to assume the identity of Sherringham. He found occasion to say that he had always, until Miriam, thought himself above all moral dilemmas, a man too well-settled in his career to do less than condemn, even if mildly, others less well-settled than himself. Lucian too confessed in Sherringham's name, saying that in succumbing to Miriam's charms, he had done a double wrong, sacrificing as he did even the honor of his sister, Julia.

Edgar answered Max? Donald? Lucian? Victoria's smile?—Chester could not determine. He confessed to lust in the name of Gabriel Nash, making of the esthete a great masturbator, saying: "I never have to visualize the face or body of another person. I can masturbate quite successfully without conjuring up any image at all, satisfied by the purely tactile. Which leads me to believe that the single important thing in sex is the tactile, and what difference, except perhaps a perverse one, if a second person holds your . . . ?"

Lucian insisted that Edgar be awarded a Grace Card.

Chester, of course, ignored Lucian and he issued a penalty to Edgar.

Victoria, describing Miriam's relationship to Sherringham, chose—perhaps for what she thought of as the humor of it—to fix Sherringham's identity on the poet, Donald Marwel. It should be mentioned that even as she kept a light tone to her confessions, she developed a black if sarcastic picture of Miriam, intimating that Miriam was capable of lying and cheating, passionate, through misdirected energy, to hurt others and to have her way.

Emily, as if set straight by the false direction of Victoria's confession, as if now seeing the possibility of there being two Sherringhams at the board, said haughtily, in Julia's name, that she would never forgive her brother for nearly sacrificing his career for a strumpet. Oh yes, she would receive him. But she would stare unflinchingly into his eyes until shame made him turn away.

Donald perhaps felt himself in the clear. And he switched identities now, from Sherringham to Gabriel Nash. He had not the wit of a nash; he made up for that with a most clear logic. Nash was, for him, the perpetual observer who would watch the moral degeneration of another with a smile. Was there not in Donald's interpretation of Nash a bit of Edgar? Max? Lucian? Was there not a Marwel as well?

Robinson, putting a period to Miriam's youth, described her meetings and relations with Basil Dashwood. Once, he had been full of life and hope, a sort of Sir Galahad in search of a sort of Holy Grail. But in his travels, he had found no grail, and had incurred debts, for traveling, she said, could be very expensive. Debts to this one and that.

Debts of all sorts. Written on his face when she met him, he then wretched, on the road to ruin. She confessed sadly, her head bent, though, from time to time, she glanced out the corner of her eye at Luther who, smiling, not looking at her, nodded to her words. She, she continued, on the very doorstep of success, had fallen in love with him, with his despair, with the idea of a man who had sunk so low. Attracted to him, she claimed, as to an alternative to the Nashes who people the salons of success. And Basil, poor Basil, had sold her to Nash, to ugly Nash. Was it to pay back a debt? Was it a gesture to free her of him? In any event—her voice low, becoming a bit bitter—she had betrayed not Basil, but her love, the very best in her, and had gone, yes, Basil at her side, to the hotel Nash was stopping at.

Luther then volubly confessed that it was true, he had sold Miriam to Nash. Oh, he was a sinner. He had, even as Miriam had said, spent everything. Like water. Max Wise smilingly modified Robinson's facts, saying that he had taken Miriam from Basil not as repayment, but only as interest on a loan. Luther laughed. And Edgar, as Nash, said that what he had done with Basil, he had done for the best. Had he not accomplished the reformation of Basil's character? For Basil had learned—had he not?—to turn the other cheek. He had taught him humility. What a quality for a nineteenth century man!

* * *

Charles Rizzo's Gabriel Nash had been developed in such a way that he could now say: "In Samarcand, where I have spent much time, man lives only by art—that is, certain men, the men of interest. And so, the painter, my friend, the ascetic Ahmed ben Yussef, known throughout his country as a judge (for his art is, even as art must always be, a personal, a secret affair), would subordinate even justice to art. Having condemned a thief to having his hand lopped off, he would, from his window overlooking the courtyard, arrange the spectacle, call out his orders to his guards—to move to the right, one in the shadows of the terrible instrument that would execute the judgment, another kneeling before the thief in a tableau as impermanent and perpetual as art itself. And I, at the side of my hawk-nosed friend, participated in such rites. Shall I deny my pleasure?"

Donald, as Gabriel Nash, tried to insert reason into the game. He said that when one hurts another, one hurts, I fear, oneself most of all. He described how he, in interfering in the lives of Miriam, Nick, Sherringham, and Basil too, had perhaps done irreparable damage. And to himself.

Lucian was now Basil. And it was true he would not condemn Miriam for her peregrinations. She was a superior person; he would turn the other cheek.

* * *

Robinson's Miriam had arrived on stage. She spoke now with confidence and poise, sure of her voice and art. And if, by a smile, by a catch in her voice, she reminded one of the Miriam of just a few confessions before, the smile or catch came across as technique, a fillip to her art. Modesty, timidity, were young Miriam's properties; but Miriam, the actress, was mistress of herself.

"At three in the afternoon, because the light is as it is at that hour, I had Basil fetch a *fiacre* and we drove to Carleton Mews where Mr. Nicholas Dormer, the painter, had his studio. I left poor Basil in the *fiacre*, saying only, 'I'll be just a minute, dear.'

"Mr. Dormer was waiting for me, busy preparing his palette, his easel. Greeting me, he smiled, but he was upset for it was to be a painting in the nude, upset that he would have to lock the door of his studio. For art, poor fellow. And I, for art, removed my clothes behind a screen he had considerately arranged for me; and he, for art, would not look until I had taken the pose we had previously decided on, on a pedestal, he to represent me as the tragic muse. And so it was. He lost himself in his work, in his examination of me as the muse, a finger at my lips, smiling faintly. He worked at length, doing his portrait that would be his masterpiece. And strangely, I was glad for the discomforts of my pose, as if, in holding the pose, I was more the artist than him. But then, I grew envious. It was, after all, a gift, my posing, and what did I really care about having my portrait done? Besides, I was hot—poor Basil waiting outside for me. And I moved my leg a twitch which upset Nick a bit, and did I then smile in that twisted way I sometimes have? My tactic was to move by less than inches, each move to make him confuse line and color . . ."

Victoria, going out of turn, threw the dice, and but barely regarding the sin she landed on, said: "How dramatic you make me appear, Jane. Really, the studio scene was as simple as pie. Nick was the trembling type and that's the only reason it took so long. Why think of it; the portrait was never even begun. And if there was art involved, it was only in my pose: the tragic muse. No. Nick was only playing with his paints while I thought he was doing my portrait, nervously playing until I gave him a wink."

Robinson was hiding a smile.

Edgar laughed outright.

And Chester shrugged.

*   *   *

Luther said that it was true that he had learned humility, chastened like an unruly boy. It was true, he continued, that the truth will make you free. But, he added, smiling strangely, who has control over the truth? Some people believe that the truth's in here, he said, pointing to his gut. Some people believe that the truth's a fist. But what if the truth's only the light inside your eyes when you close your eyes hard. Light and only light. When you press your eyes so tightly shut that you see white, glowing hot white. Maybe it's true that if you hurt someone else, you hurt yourself. But what if, all in all, the truth's a lie?

*   *   *

Edgar gave his own version of Miriam's visit to Nick Dormer's studio. But, confessing as Nick Dormer, was he himself? In any event, he said that he had wanted to capture the oriental attraction, the sensuality, of Miriam on canvas and he had had her pose for him. The painting was nearly accomplished when Julia, without knocking, entered. She stood, proud, in silence, all the while he painted, jealous less of the events she might have imagined than of the sensuality of Miriam. Furious that he, Nick, could be subject to such charms.

Emily confessed at length in Julia's name, saying, in effect, that it was not sensuality but youth that was the subject of the painting.

Victoria, as Miriam, confessed to betraying Basil. She made the confession with evident satisfaction, and in her voice was a certain admiration for Miriam.

In short, the evening ended unpleasantly and in much confusion.

6

Max offered to get a chicken and Victoria said yes, she would wait. She locked the door after him and drowsed off in his bed. Max returned with a paprika-sprinkled, barbecued chicken, and Victoria, in Max's too large robe, sat on the edge of the bed, he in a chair across a small table from her, neon lights from outside playing garishly, intimately, over everything in the room. They ate the chicken with their fingers, the grease polishing their lips. When they had finished, Victoria offered one end of the wishbone to Max and even if he smiled in that way he had—an answer perhaps to her own smile—they broke the bone together.

Sometimes, he brought back as well a bottle of wine.

One Sunday morning, Victoria called Max and suggested they go for a drive.

They met outside her building; Peregrine Moth was waiting. Victoria asked Max if he would like to drive. Evidently, he was not an experienced driver; she had to show him the gear positions; he stalled once or twice. He drove to 125th Street and turned east through Harlem. Here were shops, bars, barbershops, movie theatres one after the other, bare in the day for lack of neon. Colored men and women, their gross features alike, lounged restlessly in groups; an early drunk weaved his way along the street.

They drove to the Triborough Bridge and onto it. Looking back, Victoria saw a bit of the New York skyline. She thought of approaching the city by airplane, at night, at dawn; the sun rising in the windows of the city buildings, and then, as you drove in a cab in the city, the tumultuous awakening, the chaotic movement, industry. A monk—had he been a Cistercian?—had said in the course of a tour he had guided through his monastery in Provence that the intellect is vertical and the heart is horizontal. Of course, he was a sentimentalist—his center teeth missing, and his faint, gentle halo of hair. But how grand towers could be, rising, piercing. Gothic and Romanesque; gargoyles and pure, simple lines.

They were on a boulevard she vaguely remembered from years before, before the network of west side highways, when the East Bronx had been a fast way to Connecticut. They passed fifty used car lots, advertising billboards. Then, they were in a residential neighborhood and Max was driving at a snail's pace so that Victoria realized he was showing her his Bronx. Here and there were six-story squat apartment buildings that once, perhaps, had bordered on respectability. Now, the area was all Puerto Rican save for a few Jewish shops. Max pointed out a ground floor apartment and said that he had lived there until he was eighteen, when his mother had died. He pointed out an orange brick synagogue. His grandfather, he said, had been one of its "founding fathers." He had come from Russia, aged sixty-five, and elegant in white beard and derby hat, grey and black striped trousers and black coat, had, carrying a silver knobbed walking stick, walked every morning and evening to the synagogue—a sight for poor children. He poked fun at the old man's pretensions, perhaps, Victoria thought, afraid that she would otherwise laugh not at the grandfather but at him. It was all one to her. She liked the image, the absurdity of a man dressed that way in this neighborhood, the pride involved.

Now, Victoria at the wheel, Peregrine Moth outside the city on familiar parkways, just fine at fifty-five, and Max at her side, quiet, like a stranger to whom she had given a lift. So dark. Perhaps he was thinking of his Bronx; he was distant, lost in his thoughts.

She drove north; it was her direction and it was like being cleansed. By the air which rushed in cool through the side vents and half-open windows. The trees lining the parkway; the autumn colors—rust red and rust yellow. Now, up the gravel driveway, slowly, she a child at her bedroom window. The evenings when there had been five cars in the driveway: musicians—amateurs, invited professionals. The music had lingered. So that, a day or two later, at her spot at the waterfall, far from the house, she had heard the music distant but clear.

They walked; she led—on tiptoe because she wore heels, he with his hands clasped behind his back. A thorn scratched a run in her stocking and she stopped in a grove of pine to remove stockings and shoes; she glanced up at him—he was mopping his forehead with a handkerchief, looking up towards the spaces between the trees the way some people, when they enter an apartment, look immediately for the window. They continued on towards the lake, the boathouse there, she barefoot now, carrying her shoes.

"I used to come here often," Victoria offered.

Max smiled in that way of his.

"Can you row?" she asked.

He removed his jacket as she loosened the ropes that tied the boat to. He pushed off awkwardly, the boat emerging into the warm afternoon light, onto the very placid lake. A small lake; great water lily leaves lapped against the sides of the boat. In the center of the lake, the water clear, Max lifted the oars into the boat and let the boat drift. He shifted his seat, she at the bow, he now at the stern, his eyes closed, receiving the sun. She let her hand hang in the water and she drifted off, the way one can in the sun.

She felt Max stirring at the other end of the boat, perhaps nervous now that he had taken the sun, in the nothing-to-do-ness. How wrong he was here. But she felt an enormous lassitude, a generosity of spirit. She opened her eyes and would have smiled nicely. She was sure Max was posing for her—his head held back, chin-up, he reptilian in the sun. She thought then that here, in full light, he was not a person; he was a multitude. He smelled of people and of the city.

And yet, there was the silence. There was, when she again closed her eyes and let herself drift in the warmth of the sun, a feeling of being tired with someone who was at least as tired as she. A feeling that, with eyes closed, each aware of the other, each was following his own memories with sadness. She knew that were she to look at him now, it would all fall apart; she would encounter a smile. A man was calling. She opened her eyes; Max was sitting up, his head turned towards the shore, towards the caretaker there who had not recognized Victoria and was gesturing them to return. An old man who had worked for Victoria's parents, and who, with his wife, tried to keep everything here as it had been. Victoria did not bother to make herself more visible to him than she was, nor to answer his calls. He would find her car soon enough and would recognize his mistake.

She must have slept. It was becoming cool; the shore greens were dark in the late afternoon light; the woods were filled with deep shadows and the sun struck clear the tops of trees. A slight breeze ran along the surface of the water. "Shall we go back?" Victoria said, and was not then sure what she meant by "back." The shore? The house? The drive back? The city? Not yet. Poor, noble Max, he had let her sleep. He rowed to the boathouse. Victoria tied the boat to.

"That was nice of him," Victoria said of the caretaker. He had prepared kindling and wood for a fire. She wondered if he had done so grudgingly, disapprovingly. She stood with Max in the large living room—the piano surely off-key, the fading rateen rugs woven here in Connecticut, the furniture as old and comfortable as the house, the large fireplace.

"Shall we have chicken?" Max asked.

She glanced at him quickly, close to anger. But then said, "I'll go get something and you can make the fire." After all, his irony was his manner, his very language.

She drove to the village, a few miles away. The grocer's

wife affected not to recognize her, waiting for her to make the first step. Which Victoria would not. She bought cheese and milk, hamburger and buns, mustard, tomatoes, coffee; and though she did not care for beer and did not know whether Max did, she bought a six-pack.

It was nearly dark. Driving back, she imagined Max in the house: wandering, dark and curious, through every room; finding her father's books in his study, smiling at Trollope and de Tocqueville; finding her room at the top of the house after two turns in the staircase, the ceiling inclined so that were he to stand by the window that gave on to the driveway, his head would touch the ceiling, his forehead could lean against it. How nice it was here. And the night would be clear, cold enough for quilts. The sky all bright, without a moon, she hoped, only the stars.

The fire was fine, all the room aglow with its light and shadows.

The hamburgers spit fat into the fire and soon were done. They ate; they drank milk; and though there was a gas stove in the kitchen, Victoria put a pot of water over embers for coffee. They sat in soft chairs, facing the fire, their legs stretched towards the fire.

She remembered. Each sound—of leaves rustling outside, of a creaking in the house, of a little explosion of bark in the fire—coming across at her over many years. She knew that she could not trust these memories; she had surely, if only in part, invented them herself. For her needs. She felt then as if the evening were over; there was nothing to share, not even with herself. And Max, his clothes all rumpled from the boat and sun, staring unseeing into the fire, thinking of what? Again of his Bronx? Of his parents? Had he ever been young? Honest, like me, only in the past, and nothing but inventions to hold onto. Her mind played gently, sadly, over what his past must have been, all the while she seeing the fire, hearing the noises, seeing her own memories—vague, because she would not give them credence.

"Have you seen the house?" she asked.

Wandering through it, she told him about it, its age, when this portion had been built and when the other; her parents had purchased it for her, to raise her here—simply. And she glanced at him quickly to see if he were smiling. He was looking at an old map of the region framed on a wall. Room by room; noisily, her heels; and each room was still and just a bit musty. The kitchen with copper utensils placed seemingly at random here and there so that she, with a stranger's eye, wondered at the care her parents had given to everything here. The guest bedrooms, plain; no carpeting anywhere, but a simple rug near each bed on wooden floors. To her room. Her books were in place. Her clothes. Castoffs from the last ten years of travels and schools. Smelling of mothballs. Neatly hung. Loose sweaters, skipants, boots and flats. She took a pair of flats that were curled a bit and got into them; she held a soft old sweater and decided to put that on too. She asked Max to turn around. She undressed and dressed, upsetting her hair, and just before she said he could turn again, she rubbed her hand across her lips though she had not worn lipstick that day. He looked at her, nicely, as if he were not there. She said, "I must be a sight. Would you like to change?"

He smiled then, as usual.

She said petulantly, "Oh, come on."

As if she had forgotten, Victoria went first to her mother's closet and her hand ran over the clothes there, the soft, light textures of summer things. In her father's closet was a row of business suits nearly all alike. Also, casual things: sweaters, corduroy trousers, woolen shirts, tweed jackets. Reluctantly, self-mockingly, Max took off his shirt and put on one of her father's. It fit across the chest, at the neck, but the sleeves were too long and Max had to roll them. He said of a tweed jacket that it was very handsome; it fit him only as well as the shirt.

They returned downstairs to sit by the fire.

She had sat at the piano, had struck some notes, reflectively listened as the sounds had hovered in the room. She stood and said they could sleep here, she on one sofa and he on another. Undressing, her back to him, he already lying on a sofa, she said, "If I were to tell you I like you?"

He laughed. She did too.

She felt a sudden remorse and went to him. All his hurt—if it were hurt—was twisted into a smile. She said, "Really, Max, I like you very much." Which made him laugh. So that she, playfully, angrily, slapped his face lightly. Smiling, he exclaimed, "Admirable Victoria!" He gripped her wrists hard. But she broke free and slapped him again.

7

Luther Halverson smoked a great deal of marijuana. Now and then, Edgar provided the stuff; and Robinson, though unwillingly, sometimes paid for it. Once, when Robinson was out of the room, Luther rifled her purse and found and pocketed thirty-five dollars. When Robinson discovered the loss, she made a fuss. Luther angrily denied her charges; he pleaded with her to believe him. He adopted several poses, equally transparent, equally mocking. And though Robinson began by accusing and scolding him seriously, saying what had long been in the back of her mind— "If you need money so badly, why don't you go out and get a job?"—she ended by mocking him, half-sympathetic towards him, an accomplice who would enjoy with him the taste of the stolen thirty-five dollars. She was, she thought, becoming schizophrenic. She called Luther "Basil," first angrily, then mockingly, unsure what she wanted of him. She said, "You should sell your car. What do you need it for anyway? We're not going anyplace. Not yet. I'll go with you wherever you like, to Timbuctoo, but not now. Tomorrow. And we can buy another when we go."

She said, "I'll buy the car from you. Then, it'll be like in the family."

He said that his car would not work for her.

She reminded him that it already had.

That she called him Basil only added to Luther's feelings of having power in secret, a cache of weapons below the surface. She fixed the mask of Basil onto him and so much the better. High, he invented a conceit: he and everyone he knew had been transformed by Circe into swine. He would destroy Circe. But who was she? He saw her in Robinson, in Max, in Edgar. But they too had been transformed. The genius of Circe was to make everyone resemble her, to give everyone her powers and villainy.

He began his Western.

When Robinson asked him about it, he told her that everything was coming clear. But, in truth, all he had written was: "One hot and dry day, a tall stranger rode into the town of Marcus Cross." He saw the novel. The tall stranger, by principle opposed to violence, was unarmed in this impoverished town in a rich and fertile country, his hands already—this not to be mentioned, but only felt—stained with blood. In the course of the book, the mystery surrounding the tall stranger's background would grow; he would reveal himself only in his silences; he would befriend the poor homesteaders; he would suffer the insults of the outlaw cattlemen, their slaps and laughter; he would hear himself called a coward; even by his new friends. And then,

not for himself but for the homesteaders, he would go beyond principle and would act. In a bar of stark appearance,
he would of a sudden spring into action, like lightning, an
angel of destruction destroying the outlaws, his guns blast-
ing them dead: one behind the bar, another on a staircase
overhead, and then the worst of the lot, all dressed in black,
a faceless hired gunman, shot in the neck like a snake before
he could even accomplish his draw. Then, the stranger,
wounded—who should say how seriously? for he is and has
always been tight-lipped—leaves the town, rides off into
the mountains, bloodstained again, not waiting for the
thanks of the homesteaders who will watch him with silent
emotion, his white horse, he slumped in the saddle against
the twilight.

But though he could see his scenes, even with wonderful
clarity, Luther made no progress. And the next time Robinson asked him about his work, he said it was finished. She
congratulated him. She said that now he would not have to
sell his car, that now, when he received his money, she
would pack her bags, leave college, and go with him.
"Right?"

His Jaguar was his best friend. Often now, Luther
would sit in it, parked, his hands on the wheel. Once Robinson saw him that way. She stood in shadows, watching
him, saddened, on the verge of laughter. She approached
and said, "Hi. Where've you been?"

"Frisco," he answered.

"Nice there?"

"Crazy."

From time to time, Edgar appeared at the apartment.
The apartment was, if anything, more disorderly than it

had been. Though Max no longer appeared here, his mattress was still in a corner of the room; the place had not been cleaned or dusted in ages. They rarely put on the lights, street lamps outside providing all the light anyone needed; and the room, with windows only partially open, was flooded with the rotten-sweet odor of marijuana. Luther was on his bed; Robinson was seated near him on the bed, but all her attention was directed to Edgar. He, sitting forward in the soft chair, his hat laid carelessly on the floor at his side, was holding forth. Smoking, he used the cigarette as, in another place, he might a *petit four*, holding it delicately between thumb and forefinger, now and then putting it down, now and then touching it to his lips.

"How shall I describe Barbara? She is not black, only her hair which is richly so, she being a rather dark tan. Tall, taller than you. And Timmy is the lad's name. Just three or four years old, with curly black hair and lighter of complexion than his mother so that one wonders whether the father is Caucasian. The first time I went with Barbara, I was shocked to see the lad—he in a crib at the foot of the bed. And having gazed at him, sleeping, his thumb in his mouth, a toy car in the other hand, having gazed at the room—a whore's room in a cheap hotel, soaps and bottles of lavender waters, gargling water—an after-dinner drink to a trip around the world (see, Luther, I am a great voyager)—I felt a spark of conscience and would have left. But Barbara was already at the sink, washing herself there, such a pleasant, such a conjugal scene—mother at the sink and child asleep in his crib—that I decided that I might, without troubling myself further, remain.

"In the midst of Barbara's endeavors, Timmy awoke. He did so silently and rose in his crib, his chin barely reaching the edge of the bed. Barbara, industrious, conscientious soul, was doing her best, then at—shall I say?—Trinidad in the Southern Hemisphere, and did not see her child. I did, and though at first I lost spirit, I then winked at the child, who, like his mother, had a singular *sang-froid*, sucking his thumb, holding his car. When I left, I hasten for your better thoughts of me to add, I, having already paid the mother a decent wage, gave to her a second bill of like denomination and said, 'This is for the child, to buy him a toy.' "

Robinson said admiringly, "How ugly you've become."

Sometimes, Luther smiled to himself; sometimes, he spoke up. But he rarely knew when. That was funny. Because sometimes, he looked up at them for a reaction to something he had said, but there was none. So that he wondered if he had said anything at all. And sometimes, they looked at him with amusement, condescendingly, mockingly, their own conversation halted, he wondering at that because he was sure his previous thoughts had been silent. This high, his mind was absolutely clear and his every thought was true, only he did not know when he uttered them. "Have I ever told you about my friend, Llewellyn? We went together on weekend retreats. When we were kids. And we'd speak about god and how one should live. We were pure. I was a runner. A hundred yard man. A burst of energy from beginning to finish. In tents in the country, in lake country. And climbing trees and swimming. Only, the Devil was there. We both knew it. Llewellyn could even see the Devil in a bottle of Coca Cola. And ten years later, I read that Llewellyn was wanted by the police in Minnesota for flagellation. His wife, to make her pure. She thought it hurt and made a complaint. He? I don't think they ever got him. He probably went up north, to Manitoba, to one of those sects, and is flagellating still. Have you ever been to a Sauna? We should go. It's fun."

"I'd like you to call me Barbara," Robinson said.
"Not Timmy?" Edgar asked.
"You *are* terrible."
"But what fun—growing up."
"Fun for you, misery for me," she said in a childish voice.

The floor was slippery with moisture; the room was filled with white clouds of steam behind which one could hide for an instant. Perspiration dripped from Robinson's hair, down all her body; her lips were swollen, partly open in a half-afraid, half-expectant smile; and, as Luther tested his birch switch, making it whistle through the steam, making it crack with a twist of his wrist, she put her hands in front of her, modestly, suggestively, protecting her private parts. Edgar sat on a bench, smiling condescendingly, waiting to see, his flesh all rosy and flabby. And Luther, though he took a step towards Robinson, turned suddenly and struck at Edgar. Who stood, shielding his face with his arms, so that the birch, once and again, hit his forearms, leaving its imprint all red there. Who laughed as Luther continued, twisting this way and that as if tickled, turning about on his toes, drawing his neck into his shoulders, laughing uncontrollably. Robinson too had found a switch and as Luther pursued Edgar, she pursued Luther, all three of them laughing, each in his own way, Luther feeling Robinson's blows only enough to give an added twist to his switch which cracked explosions through the clouds Edgar tried to hide behind.

8

The Wolgamuts, it had been arranged not long after their last evening, would next meet on a Friday at Victoria's home in Connecticut. Victoria had, in fact, invited them all for the weekend. Also, it had been decided that they would use Jane Austen's *Pride and Prejudice* as a context for the Game of Dostoevsky.

Expecting that it would require much work to prepare her house for a Wolgamut weekend, Victoria had, by phone, hired the caretaker's wife to help her maid. But when Victoria arrived in Connecticut and detailed to the caretaker's wife, a stout, grey-haired woman, what was expected of her, the caretaker's wife looked meaningfully at Victoria's maid and said that *she* was no slave. It was early in the morning; Victoria called an agency for domestics in New York and was promised that a maid would be sent up to her shortly. Later, Victoria went to the village, did a great deal of shopping, and then met the train arriving from the city.

The people descending were Negroes, maids all. They carried little sacks; some wore clothes too big, too small, or too *chic* for them. Victoria alone stood waiting in their midst on the platform; the other employers sat in their automobiles, now and then honking their horns. There was but one Negro left on the platform, ugly, peevish-looking, perhaps twenty-five years old, and Victoria approached her. In Peregrine Moth, the maid said that she had rushed so much, she had not had time for breakfast. It was, in fact, nearly lunchtime before she got to work; and she worked slowly, in a slovenly way. Victoria would have sent her back to the city, but she knew she would not be able to get a replacement before the following morning and ten guests would be arriving this evening. She was saddled with the girl and it irritated her. The girl complained that she was cold. Victoria asked her if she had not brought a sweater. She answered that in the city, the apartments she worked in were always well-heated. That, Victoria had not thought of. She had envisaged a fine wood fire. How foolish, for her guests would require regular heating if only for the hot water. She phoned the caretaker; he was out and she asked his wife if her husband could not get the heating system, a coal burner, going. The wife said smugly that the burner had not been looked at in years, that there was no coal. Victoria said that her husband would have the burner working within four hours and she hung up.

Throughout the day, there was no let-up for Victoria. There were a thousand and one things to be done; from

towels and washcloths for each guest to flowers for the
women and cigarettes which she had forgotten to buy. De-
livery men arrived. Everything had to be put in place; she
had to check on the new girl, plan for weekend entertainments. Tomorrow morning, some of the guests might go
horseback riding, others might go boating, walking; or,
might stay in the house, by the fire, reading, listening to
music. The phonograph was an old, ornate thing; the records were all seventy-eight rpms, in numbered albums cata-
loged by her father. And she? She would go riding with
Chester, to the village with Robinson's bearded friend, and
Sunday morning to church with Max.

The house was in order, dinner was being prepared,
when the first guests arrived: Chester Mawr, Simon Parr,
Lucian Whittier, Charles Rizzo and Max Wise. They had
met on the train coming up from the city, had shared a cab
from the station, and if all was not friendship between
them, then most was pleasant antipathy, ironical, oblique
conversation. Victoria had had a minute to freshen up and
change and she bowed her head to them now in an excess
of modesty and maidenliness and said, "My father is expecting you. You are the insurance gentlemen, aren't you?"
    They were, in fact, all in dark suits, and though Lucian
and Simon each had a small suitcase, the others carried
briefcases. Chester smiled and said: "I am Mr. Mawr of
Underwriting; the tall gentleman is Mr. Parr of Overwrit-
ing; this is our new colleague, Mr. Wise of Accidents and
Disasters; and Mr. Whittier and Mr. Rizzo there are of
Consolation and Commiseration."

Victoria had just shown them to their rooms when the
Marwels arrived. She could hardly meet them in the same

spirit. The poet and his wife entered with smiles and light
baggage, the perfect guests, immediately finding something
to compliment Victoria on—she the perfect hostess—the
stairway for its proportions. Max came down the stairs.
Victoria said, "Max dear, would you please do the fire?
Max, you know," she said to the Marwels, "already is familiar with the house."

She showed the Marwels to their rooms. She heard a car
pulling up in the driveway. And descending again, she
smiled seeing Lucian, in profile, at a window in the entranceway. The Fine Arts Instructor had changed and
wore a tweed jacket cut a bit wide at the shoulders, narrow
at the waist—in the English style. He wore flannel trousers,
a pale blue shirt, and an Ascot in place of a necktie. He
announced, "Three in a Jaguar: Mr. Hope, the bearded
one, and charming Miss Robinson. Miss Robinson is at the
wheel; Mr. Hope is smiling thinly as if he has just under-
gone a threatening experience; but the other one, cradled
between them, seems not at all the worse for the experience, smiling like a child. But now, what's this? What fran-
tic activity? She brushes her hair—so attractively wind-
swept; she powders her nose, laughing a bit. Mr. Hope puts
on his hat, carefully gives it a rakish tilt. Now, both con-
verge on the other, one putting a handkerchief into his
breast pocket, the other fitting a cigarette into his mouth.
Ah, the entrance."

Robinson wore a simple dress. Her manner was gentle,
timorous, she seemingly embarrassed, as if by the company
she arrived in. Luther Halverson was evidently high. He
had a most serene smile. His eyes were wide open, studying
as he entered, all things, seeing, it seemed, nothing at all.
And Edgar, stout and handsome, nodded to Lucian and
bowed to Victoria whom he called, "Dear Miss Bennet"—

surely identifying her as the wise heroine of *Pride and Prejudice*. He introduced Robinson as Mrs. Charlotte Collins—a reasonable but perhaps insufficiently proud and daring character of the novel in question. Luther was Mr. Wickham, "or at least, the shadow of Mr. Wickham"—the gay and irresponsible scoundrel of the novel. And Edgar was the novel's hero, the proud Darcy.

Lucian said that a mistake had been made, that he was Mr. Wickham.

Victoria said that they were fortunate to have in the house several insurance agents who would, in time, proceed to proper verifications of identity.

Chester and Victoria sat at the head and foot of the long and crowded dining room table. Emily Marwel sat center, facing Robinson. Luther was at Edgar's left and faced Max who was at Donald's right. And Lucian was at Victoria's left and faced Simon and Charles. The two maids did the serving.

Chester found early occasion to say, like a blessing, that he would never have dreamed of making this journey into the wilderness had he not known that Victoria would be waiting for him. He spoke then, cleverly, but good-humoredly, of the charms of country living.

Victoria listed the things her guests might do during the weekend.

Emily said, "I will go boating. But I will want a parasol and many admirers."

Robinson said that she would go riding, if she could find a stable companion.

Many were riders.

Lucian lightly reproached Victoria that had he known

there would be riding, he would have brought along riding clothes.

"And you, the false Mr. Wickham," Lucian asked Luther, "do you ride?"

Luther smiled and said that he rode to the hounds.

Replenishing his glass, Edgar playfully cautioned the group, saying: "Thanks to Mr. Wise, I have come to a thorough and needed reappraisal of Jane Austen. And in my reappraisal, I give great prominence to Jane's lucidity. For, above all else, Jane is lucid. There's the rub. Lucid as she is, is it conceivable that she was not more aware than she seems to be of the—shall we say?—viciousness of her generation? Ah, she hints at it. She demands not just a new reading, but a new writing; each hint, nicely developed, would be an illumination, a chapter."

"My dear Edgar," Chester said, "if the result of your reappraisal is that Jane has a dark side, I can't imagine what your thesis resembled until now."

"It was a nice thing," Edgar smilingly replied. "I admired Jane's sense of form, the structure of her works, the clarity of what I thought of as her limited vision."

"And so you should still," Chester said. "The form. The structure. As for the dark side, that should have been clear to you long ago. Nor for you now, under the Russian influence, to divulge the full meaning behind a glance, a phrase, but, to be even as discreet as Miss Austen, and to hint, in your thesis, even as she in her novel, of those darker elements."

"But why only hint?" Edgar asked, continuing the conversation that Chester thought he had closed. "Should we not bring all of Jane into the light? The details of her thought, of her vision of the world. If only to clarify, and then, clarified, to appreciate more the subtilty of her art. Of course, I have no intention of publishing my thesis, that would be putting a weapon into the hands of the uninitiated; but, after all, among ourselves? In any event, I am learning so much in writing my thesis that I feel I cannot stop now, not until *I* have plumbed all of Jane's depths. Think, for example, of Lydia, of the way she is characterized. Is it not so that in another novel, she would be described in bed? Should we not see her in bed? How she reacts to the experience. How she adds to the experience. Wickham is a gambler. Should we not be told of his feelings at the table? Ah, that subject is dealt with elsewhere. But doesn't it seem that Jane jealously keeps those experiences to herself? So that one can even imagine her nights— she thrilling over Wickham losing money he does not have, thrilling over the darker plots she but hints at in the daytime. And the bed scene of Darcy and Elizabeth. Details! Doesn't that scene merit a chapter, perhaps a book?"

"Why?" Chester asked.

"Pardon?"

"Would such a scene add anything? You have, after all, the hint."

"Why it would add to my sensations. I should hope it would satisfy me the more."

"And that, of course, makes anything worthwhile?"

"You pose a serious question," Edgar said, smiling.

A light conversation began over Donald Marwel's newest poem, *Sabbatical.*

It is a fairly long poem in which a teacher, after seven long and tedious years at a university, searches for a renewal of all his romantic notions in the Greek islands and in "Byzantium." Passing the island of Icaria, he thinks of

Icarus striving for the sun. But arriving in Byzantium, he discovers only violence and poverty. He is attacked; the images are of a physical attack; it could, as well, be an attack on the spirit. In any event, in a remarkably slow last stanza, the teacher is just coming to himself in a room one might easily think of as being in an asylum. He is, one gathers, cured of his illusions. He slowly turns 'the loose-leaves of time.'

Some saw something of Edgar in the teacher.

Simon was a bit insulted that no one saw him as the poem's hero. After all, the trip had been his. And who else had been attacked?

Donald said mildly that the poem's subject was general.

"I had thought," Robinson said in the character of Charlotte Collins, "that it was an ungenerous attack on Mr. Wickham."

"Do you mean the real or the false Mr. Wickham?" Lucian asked.

"What does the real Mr. Wickham think?" Edgar asked Luther.

"What?" Luther asked. He had not heard the question. He smiled in a puzzled way.

"Oh he," Lucian said, "is more a wickless than a wickham."

Luther excused himself before dinner was over. He had grown somewhat pale. He left the dining room, but perhaps five minutes later reappeared, occasioning some mirth. Robinson said she would put him to bed and return.

Dinner was not over until late and the Wolgamuts decided to retire early and play the Game of Dostoevsky the following evening. They sat in the living room, which, as has been mentioned was large, almost as large as the hall of

Victoria's apartment in the city. But the dim light here, the wood paneling, the wooden floor, the low ceiling, and above all, the fireplace with a fine fire flaming, made the room seem intimate and warm. There was cognac and scotch. Simon Parr operated the phonograph; as the records were all short-play, he remained by the machine. He went one by one through an album of Mozart horn works.

Victoria felt, from time to time, Max's eyes on her. Alone, in a corner of the sofa opposite, he was wondering, she knew, how he would come to her this night. She spoke with Chester Mawr, the penguin-shaped man comfortably seated in an armchair, warming his brandy glass in his hands. Of an Italian liner they had each, more than once, sailed on, and which had sunk some years before. It had been a beautiful ship and they spoke with the sadness and nostalgia of people just accustoming themselves to their grief. The conversation faded into another. Victoria liked talking to Chester, looking in on the others. Lucian was close by with Jane Robinson; he called her Mrs. Collins; she addressed him as Mr. Wickham Question Mark. Charles, like Darcy in an early scene of the novel, kept very much to himself. He sat for a time at a table, writing a letter. And Edgar, a more voluble Darcy—perhaps one culled from those unwritten chapters—stood, at some distance from Victoria, with the Marwels. He dominated that conversation as he had had the one with Chester at dinner, and his words, if one could judge from Emily's frequent smiles, were no less nuanced. He glanced at Victoria, smiling a nuanced invitation. She turned from the smile to Chester, asking abruptly, dispensing with the conversation at hand, "Doesn't Max go well with the fire?"

Chester answered, "If you think so, Victoria."

His tone was perhaps a result of her rudeness. She

would, nevertheless, not continue with him. She called Max to her. Even at her call, Lucian came, leaving Robinson. And while Max stood waiting, smiling in that way of his, Lucian knelt at her feet and said, "Won't you play for us, Miss Bennet?"

"The piano is off-key," she said.

"All the more reason," Lucian said.

"You play," she said, gaily now.

Lucian went to the piano.

Victoria looked up at Max and said, "Oh, I've forgotten what I wanted to tell you."

"It'll wait until later," Max said.

Lucian played gently, gracefully, and though the piano was off-key, he seemed impervious to that. In fact, there were times when the off-notes fell so amusingly that Victoria thought they had been planned for.

*　　*　　*

Victoria was in her room; all the guests had retired. She lit a candle and went halfway down a flight of stairs. Max was at her side. Prone, she did not see his face in the dark and she ran her fingers over his features. It was her private game of "Who Are You?" For the rest, their only variation that night was to tease the silence.

In the morning, she awoke fresh to a cock's crow. It was past dawn and the sky promised clear weather. She searched for an idea that had made her smile just before she had fallen asleep. Lucian. She would find him a riding habit.

Lucian had somehow arranged her father's clothes to fit him well. He wore his English-style jacket and his Ascot of the previous evening and he looked quite the rider. Edgar, Robinson and Charles were also in riding clothes, though theirs had been less nicely selected. Victoria gave them directions for a stable close-by and told them she would join them later. She wore jodhpurs and soft boots. Emily, in a large straw hat Victoria had found for her, said she would go boating, posing her statement as an invitation. Max said he would stay in the house and read; and Simon Parr, surely more innocently, said that he would too. Since neither Chester or Luther had yet appeared, Emily was obliged to be satisfied with but her husband for admirer. Victoria accompanied them to the boathouse.

It was a lovely day, and leaving the Marwels, Victoria cracked a twig from a tree and walking parallel to the lake in a shortcut to the stable, switched the twig indifferently before her. She saw someone swimming. She saw only his shoulders and arms—a strong swimmer swimming with ease and a nice stroke. She stepped behind a tree that she should not be observed; she cupped her hand to her forehead to see more clearly into the sun. It was Luther Halverson. When he emerged from the water, she was not surprised to see that he wore nothing, and was saddened, remarking how he suddenly and violently began to shiver.

Lucian was an experienced rider. He outshone Edgar and Charles even as Victoria outshone Jane Robinson. Sometimes, Victoria and Lucian were far ahead of the others. It pleased her to feel the air rushing against her skin, to feel her fine control of her mount. And it pleased her too to know that Lucian was never far from her, she leading the way.

The day passed uneventfully. In the afternoon, some of the guests played croquet. Victoria sat at Chester's side on a small terrace overlooking the lawn. The older man watched the game with amusement and now and then interrupted his conversation—flowers, about which he knew quite a lot—to offer an ironic remark on the style of one or another of the players.

* * *

Chester had once been The Grand Inquisitor; Edgar too, and besides, there were some who preferred that Edgar not be The Grand Inquisitor. Donald Marwel was favored by some, but was thought by others to be too reasonable to allow for much fun. Edgar suggested Wickham. Lucian said that he would prefer to make his own defense. Edgar said that he had meant the real Wickham. That aroused smiles. Jane Robinson, in the character of Charlotte Collins, said that it was not correct the way they treated poor Wickham. Lucian promised to defend him in the game.

Of course, what was required for The Grand Inquisitor, as Chester then indicated—smiling ruefully, perhaps at his pun—was the sense and sensibility of Victoria. Victoria accepted the compliment and responsibility, taking her place in an armchair behind the board, facing into the fire. The board was enclosed between two sofas. The players found places on the sofas and on cushions on the floor.

Chester was at the end of a sofa, close to Victoria. He began the game, confessing in the name of clever but inefficacious Mr. Bennet, the father of Elizabeth Bennet, the heroine of *Pride and Prejudice*. The next to throw the dice was Emily Marwel, and she, holding in her lap the large straw hat Victoria had given her in the morning—as if it would go with her role—confessed in the name of Lydia Bennet, the younger, flighty, flirtacious, and finally semi-ruined sister of Elizabeth Bennet. Next was Donald who confessed now in the name of one character and would later confess in the name of another.

Jane Robinson, at the far end of the board, seated modestly on a cushion, confessed, as was expected, in the name of Charlotte Collins.

Edgar, at her side, was Darcy.

Max was at the far end of the second sofa and he said he would confess in the name of Jonathan Stubbs.

"Pardon?" Victoria said.

"Chapter Twelve," Max said. " '. . . A soldier had been flogged.' "

Victoria smiled and said that Max might confess.

Max said that he, Jonathan Stubbs, had been a poor boy. Nevertheless, he had been a third to Darcy and Wickham at Darcy's home, Pemberley. Young with them if of another class, caddying for them as it were.

Charles, at Max's side, was a second Darcy.

Luther Halverson, leaning far back into the sofa, at almost as great a distance from the game as Victoria, was no one. He was very far gone, all alone with a serene smile. Victoria was lenient to him, asking, when it was his turn, if he would like to confess. She was but half humoring him.

Lucian, seated below Victoria, confessed in the name of Wickham. He said that Darcy had been born rich and he had been born no more than well. He was, he supposed, guilty of envy. He was, as well, guilty of pride—that he thought himself as good as Darcy.

Simon was at Lucian's right and he wandered about the book, now a country gentleman, now an officer, now wearing the cloth. Victoria thought that he had probably, before this evening, written down, listing them, characters and events beneath each of the seven sins. In any event, he was about the only player to, when he landed on a sin, feel obliged to make a confession truly pertinent to that sin.

* * *

Emily's Lydia Bennet was full of animal spirits. She lacked reasonableness. She had a sweet tooth and stole sugared candies in the middle of the night. She was egotistical and thought rarely, if ever, of others.

Jane Robinson's Charlotte Collins was, in her early years, not unlike Jane's version of Miriam of *The Tragic Muse*. Decent, timorous, unhappy. She described her taste for romantic tales, the disparity between her imaginative life and her adventureless real life. She admired heroes; she read mythology; Icarus made her gasp with admiration.

At the beginning of the game, Edgar's Darcy was a solitary soul. Early orphaned, living in the vastness of Pemberley. Friendless, afraid of the future which, by his birth, made such great demands on him. Not for him a military career, though he might have wanted that, nor affairs where one could play for power, nor the cloth where one could establish powerful relations. But, to uphold pride and nice prejudice. To preserve the fine, to marry himself to the best of everything of his age and be, in short, the urn of tradition.

Charles Rizzo's Darcy was tall, dark, arrogant. In society, he felt but *ennui* and disdain. He was a collector of art. Pemberley was his treasure. There, all was lofty, handsome, perfection. Charles would later indicate that Darcy's attachment to Miss Elizabeth Bennet was exactly as his attachment to other fine things that inhabited Pemberley, and he would say—in a fit of pique at the author of *Pride and Prejudice*—that he did not understand how anyone could have thought that he could have tolerated the family and friends of Miss Bennet.

Was it modesty that made Donald Marwel assume the role of conventional, mediocre, Canon Collins? In any event, in the Canon's name, he was the first to mention Lady Catherine de Bourgh, his patron, a haughty woman of immense property and power and, as characterized by Donald in Canon Collins' name, a responsible person, a preserver of law and order.

Jonathan Stubbs, defining himself, even as were some others, spoke of his days at Pemberley. How could he not have admired that place and its occupants? Darcy, elegant Wickham. Think of Stubbs' sordid home, the bed he shared with three brothers, his slatternly sisters. His father was a poacher; his mother drank. And then, some days, to be permitted to serve at lofty Pemberley, permitted to glimpse Darcy's angelic sister, and, most wonderful, to feel a similarity between himself and Wickham, Wickham with a chip on his shoulder.

True, Edgar said, Wickham had always had a chip on his shoulder. Jane was too discreet to mention that, just as she was too discreet to more than hint at Stubbs' existence, or, for that matter, at my own most black tendencies, but Wickham had known, even from his childhood, that he was as if a person dispossessed. Imagine the chagrin of a youth who feels himself robbed of his heritage. Not the legacy. That is too simple. But Pemberley. As if Wickham had thought that Pemberley, at least in another life, had been his.

Lydia's Wickham was dashing. And Lydia, of animal spirits, saw and wanted.

Charlotte's Wickham appeared before her marriage to Canon Collins, he in uniform, as dashing as Lydia had described him, and full of charm. He sang true and well. And Charlotte, who had lived but half in the prosaic world, fell in love with him. It was true if unreasonable. Then, when he was most beautiful, and then, when he had not looked at her twice.

Jonathan Stubbs said that early in his life, he had joined his fortune to Wickham's. He had been his servant, his orderly in the army, his co-plotter in later life. And when Wickham had run off with Darcy's sister, had he not, in his way, shared in the pleasure?

Emily said that she had never, until Wickham, met a man who wanted to live every minute to the fullest.

Donald recounted a conversation that he had had with Lady Catherine. He salted the scene with a bit of humor, but said, in effect, that Lady Catherine was correct in her observation that young people never think of being thirty or forty years old.

Charlotte said that that was true. She had realized that and that was why she had married stable Canon Collins.

Jonathan Stubbs said that he was a witness to the following scene:

"Wickham, the fine singer, his fine tenor voice, became aware of timid Charlotte. Was it not true, Mrs. Collins, that once, when he had received from you promises, all the reason to hope, and came to your home in the dead of night, and stood in falling snow and threw a pebble to your window to tell you he was waiting, you chose, instead of joining him, to draw your curtains and pity yourself?"

Lucian said that Stubbs was mistaken. That personage in the snow was not Wickham, perhaps another.

Lydia said that Wickham was a pale, young man, with a so honest smile and yes, a lovely tenor voice. As with Charlotte, he had come to her in the dead of night; but she, unlike Charlotte, had left her family's home to go with Wickham to London.

Jane was a fine actress. Her eyes were moist. She said, "What should I have done? Gone with him to Ireland as he wanted? But don't you know, he was sick. He had consumption. My god. What would you have me do? Sit up with a dying man? Watch him cough blood?"

Edgar said that Wickham was indeed sick, not long for this world.

During these confessions, if such they could be called, Victoria looked from time to time at Luther Halverson. She thought she saw him trying to focus in on the game. Perhaps he did not understand or even hear what was being said. And his presence, perhaps, bothered only her. The others took him, his smile and silence so much for granted that it seemed their attacks were really addressed elsewhere.

Perhaps to reassert his version of Wickham, Lucian found opportunity to say that he wanted the best of everything. And, if he could have but a Charlotte and a Lydia, then he was surely guilty of something there was no name for on the board.

Chester, as Mr. Bennet, said that he was at fault in that Lydia had run off with Wickham. Abdication of authority, he called it.

*   *   *

Edgar's Darcy described Miss Elizabeth Bennet when he had first met her. He developed the Jane Austen picture of her, intimating, however, that he was giving but half the story.

Emily remarked that Elizabeth had never done Lydia justice. Her advice, for Elizabeth had always been strong on giving advice, had not taken Lydia's nature into consideration, but had been like judgments.

Jane said that Elizabeth was indeed one for giving advice. They had been such good friends, they had not had secrets from each other—or so I thought. When Wickham had told her he would come for her— that scene in the snow —she had, in her joy, gone to tell Elizabeth. And Elizabeth had told her that she had no right to throw away her life on a Wickham, to waste her life that way. Elizabeth had said, refuse him and go to Bath. You'll feel better afterwards.

"To Bath?" Victoria asked, encouraging Jane.

"Oh, you know," Jane said, "the air is milder there. You have the opportunity to look back on all things, to reflect and to understand."

Emily, as Lydia, said that she had seen Miss Bennet in London, entering a low hotel.

Donald, as Canon Collins, seemed to be trying to make of Lady Catherine and Elizabeth Bennet two faces of the same person. He described Elizabeth's pride as purely personal, a negative thing. She did not use her talents well. Lady Catherine, on the other hand, haughty as she was, sagely exercised her influence on others.

Charlotte said that it was true that Elizabeth had frequented a low London hotel. Though she hated to tattle on a friend, she too had seen her entering there, and then taking a train for Bath.

Stubbs might have been in that hotel, but noble, or perhaps not so noble Max was elsewhere. He made of Lady Catherine a woman above reproach, of clear and positive judgments. He stressed Canon Collins' role as her lackey. He said that he had been caught poaching on her land and that Lady Catherine had flogged him, thirteen lashes, and that he had felt a peculiar delight in that, an almost sensual pleasure in hating his judge.

Lucian said with seeming impatience that Stubbs had once again made a mistake. Lady Catherine had only been his judge; the army had done the flogging. He, Wickham, had done the dirty work. And if there had been pleasure for the orderly, there had been little enough, and of a passing sort, for the officer.

Max said that yes, he had been mistaken. Surely, it had been Wickham who had done the flogging.

*   *   *

Lucian had arrived at a point in his development of Wickham where he could say: "If I prefer wit and will to wisdom and caution, would it not be illogical to judge me by anything but wit and will? Therefore, when I land on 'Pride,' I will confess only to lack of pride; covetousness is a sin when one fails to obtain; lust is an excess and I acknowledge its lack of fineness; anger and gluttony are mere words; envy may be a prime virtue; and sloth . . . well, after all, there is sloth and there are the slothful."

*   *   *

Edgar had arrived at a point in his development of Darcy where he could and felt called upon to say: "All vice begins with a tip. I give a tip to this one or that, and I am given in turn a service. I give a bigger tip and I am given a bigger service. Needless to speak of human nature here. We all know about that. In short, I can buy services, which, for the sake of my confession, we will call pleasures. What is to stop me? A sense of brotherhood with Man? But who, really, is his brother's keeper? The law? But I can, in one way or another, tip the law. I am, in fact, magistrate at Pemberley. Thus, I can do as I please. And yet, pleasures have a certain progression. One is not satisfied today with a repeat of yesterday's pleasure. And risk—is it not?—is one of the greatest pleasures. I steal something. Next, I must steal something a bit bigger. And next, to increase the risk, I want to sell the stolen goods. Perhaps to the man from whom I stole. That, of course, when one is not one's own magistrate, is foolish. It could lead to prison. So, we walk a tightrope, delicately pushing pleasure to its limits.

"Now, pleasure for one as rich as myself is doubled not only by the risk, but by the difficulties in obtaining it. Too easy to buy, for example, a courtesan's charms; if one persists in that direction, it is for something more intellectual than sensual—a lesson of one sort or another. No, the single young man in possession of a good fortune, must be in want of a virgin, an unapproachable one whom, to win, he will have to do battle, do his all.

"When I first met Miss Elizabeth Bennet, I knew that my efforts here, even were they to fail, would do me honor. For, though neither Jane or I would describe her as beautiful, she was untouchable. You all remember—do you not?—my first meeting with her, when she let some others understand that she thought me arrogant (had my friend Bingham, through whose efforts I met her, told her of me?). But, my arrogance was my tactic even as her saying I was so was hers. For she saw in me, even then, the proprietor of Pemberley, and saw in Pemberley—I anticipate—a palace of pleasures.

"Surely, you all remember my meeting with Elizabeth when she was visiting Charlotte. Jane does not choose to dwell on this, but at that time, I attempted to kiss Elizabeth. She repulsed me, whetting my appetite beyond all measure, giving me to believe that my chances with her were now nil.

"In low London places, I plotted her downfall. Stubbs was never far, demonic Stubbs. He lived mainly off my tips. He poured gall into my glass, knowing it would give me pleasure. He told me that Elizabeth was his master's mistress, that she visited Wickham in a low hotel. I would not believe him; I had him flogged. But I did buy binoculars and took a room in a building opposite the hotel. And she came. And she stayed not an hour. Ah, my astonishment! My pain. But then slowly, pain turned, as it does, to pleasure, and pleasure to exquisite delight. After all, what matter virginity if its mask remains intact?

"I knew then that there was a daytime Elizabeth and a nighttime Elizabeth. They went by the same name; they were surely one and the same. Did that not give me food for thought? Why each time she was with me, chaste and untouchable, she had upon her the mark of another, another, I soon learned, more lowly even than inoffensive if peculiar Wickham. What a master of pleasure she was! Enjoying the night and in the day giving to the pleasures of the night the thrill of opposites. I set to giving her hints that I knew the worst which was the best. She understood. What games we played in the day, what subtilty to our conversation.

"In short, I asked for her hand and she accepted.

"Some might say that *Pride and Prejudice* ends here. Let

us, however, call this Chapter Sixty-Two and come to the true denouement of the novel.

"The wedding was charming. We two there in white and black, Bingham at my side, Mr. Bennet at Elizabeth's. Canon Collins performed the ceremony; Lydia was there with Wickham; Charlotte wept for joy; and Stubbs, good servant that he was, wept from the heart.

"For our wedding night, we went to Pemberley. A fine fire flaming in our bedroom there just as there is here. Elizabeth's hair was down. She wore white. She had a candle in her hand, and looking at me so tenderly, so timorously, said, 'Darcy, you will be gentle.' I nodded, clasping her warmly to me.

" 'The lights,' she said.

"I blew them out.

"I shall spare you the details, but I had for my wedding night a virgin and a whore; a child and a woman as well-versed in all the black arts as I. One minute soft as velvet, the next rasping as sand. And I met her every gesture with equal art so that we passed from pleasure to pleasure.

"But pleasure—is it not so?—is the fruit of risk. And from two in the bedroom, we went to three. And then to four and to five. And then to various bedrooms in various numbers. But risk—is it not so?—should be teased and not embraced. Therein lies the story of Elizabeth's downfall. Delighting in my partner, I parted from her, going to France, sharing my pleasures with her, even as she did hers with me, by letter; indeed performing each for the other's approbation, awaiting the post with impatience. Until, one day, risking more than I would ever dare, she organized a most immoderate pleasure. I am not sure of the details, but Stubbs was there, Wickham as well, a host of low lovers, and what have you. Orgy was rampant and scandal was the result. The word was spread abroad; our history became public. My lands were confiscated by the government; my magistrature was revoked. And Elizabeth, without a pound, fell sick. Smallpox. Perhaps contracted from what base connection. And, the book concludes on a letter I received from my friend Bingham in which, telling me how much he has been deceived by both Elizabeth and me—for he is sentimental—he informs me of Elizabeth's fate. She was scarred by the disease; one side of her face was as if burned to the bone by acid. It was said that people saw in the marks of her disease the marks of her vice."

If Victoria was pale, she was not aware of it.

She said that Elizabeth really deserved a defense, that Edgar's Elizabeth was more French than English.

Chester said that Elizabeth was a person of great warmth. In spite of herself.

"That," Victoria said arbitrarily, "is hardly a confession."

"Elizabeth," Lucian said, "has no need of a defense."

"May I," Victoria said, "confess for Elizabeth?"

She sat down at the board. But picking up the dice she then put them aside. She remained pensive a moment, smiling. And then said, "Can I really confess to a sin? Empty though complicated vessel that I am, I am guilty, I think, and only in my best moments, of boredom." Smiling still, she asked, "Can you, Mr. Darcy, or you Mr. Wickham, or you Mr. Stubbs, truly claim guilt for one of the seven sins?"

"Not I," Darcy said.

Charlotte Collins said that she could. She had felt real guilt when her cat had been run over by a *fiacre*. No one laughed, though one or two smiled.

Lydia said that she had felt guilt when, in London with Wickham, in undress in a low hotel, Darcy had entered without knocking. And why had I not felt guilt until then?

Stubbs said that he had felt guilt when, Elizabeth Bennet ravaged by disease, he had held her hand.

"Guilt at what?" Lucian asked.

"As close to guilt as I have ever been."

As it was very late, the Wolgamuts soon retired.

PART THREE
THE GAME

9

Edgar Hope was tall, heavy and handsome, his face ruddy
with good health. "Walking does the trick," he would say.
He wore a black, rakish hat, a tailored double-breasted
dark and rich grey flannel suit. He wore a black tie on a
white shirt. Engaged in conversation with Max Wise, he
held and sometimes used rhetorically his walking stick—
elegantly slender, tapered at the bottom, weighted with silver at the top where it curved sharply, like a riding crop.
He stood with his friend behind and at a short distance
from the off-white chaise longue—the wood painted
gold—which Victoria Harm was sharing with Lucian
Whittier. Charles Rizzo stood towards the center of the
hall; he faced Victoria.

On the other side of the hall, by the grand piano, its lid

raised—suggesting an inner space within the hall, a central space encompassing the big window, the chaise longue, and everyone in the hall but Edgar and Max—stood Jane Robinson and Emily and Donald Marwel. Chester Mawr and Simon Parr stood only a step or two from that group. The three men were all conventionally dressed in dark suits. The women were tall—taller, for example, than Chester—and both were lean though the poet's wife was nearly formless. Co-ed fashion, she wore a boy's button-down shirt, a skirt, and she moved and spoke—in an act—uncertainly, nervously; she brushed her dry red hair back over her forehead; she sat down on the piano bench; she stood. Jane, on the other hand, was sedate. She wore low heels, a tweed suit—a practical thing for the season.

Victoria's hair was swept back and up in a way that accentuated her high and pale brow, her large eyes—grey in the light. Her lips were faintly rouged; she wore a simple black dress. Reclining, her smile was touched with *ennui*. Lucian, seated on the chaise longue at the curve of Victoria's knees, wore, as at the last Wolgamut evening, his tweed jacket cut in the English style, an Ascot in place of a necktie. Charles wore a black suit that buttoned, like a tunic, nearly to his chin. Slender and dark, he stood quite straight, though, from time to time, he arched his back and blew some smoke towards the ceiling. He would watch the smoke—the forms it took, the place where it crossed a current of air—with the same care he but occasionally gave to Victoria and Lucian.

"Carlo," Victoria said, "do say something."

Charles smiled at her condescendingly.

Lucian said: "The other day, I saw a bald man walking

in the rain. He felt a drop on his head here, a drop there. And then, strange man, he brushed his hand back across his pate as if to brush his hair in order."

Chester was not unaware of Lucian's success with Victoria, nor of how foolish it would look for him to break with Simon—a monk (no, less than a monk) to whom, only when three, one could listen with amusement, sharing the absurdity of his most carefully considered words, his most workmanlike logic. There was, simply, no room on the chaise longue. The round man smiled wryly, feeling, in spite of himself, that he was old. For a moment, his wit made quiescent by such reflections, he allowed himself the maudlin pleasure of thinking paternalistically of some of those here; but then mocked himself for that. Hearing, not listening to Simon—his progress on his thesis, his difficulties (What? Simon in difficulties!)—he gave himself over to his own thoughts and considered that Edgar's new game was not without charm. It was, as well, in spite of the apparent freedom one had in selecting an "identity," realistic enough. For who would create or take upon himself an identity not congenial to who he was? Or, to who he would be? Emily alone. She, who perhaps thought the method of the game was parody—had Edgar purposefully given her that impression?—was miming a former Miss Robinson. Miss Robinson, understanding the mild embarrassment of the poet at his wife's lack of taste, passed the poet looks full of sympathy. Looks which, by their patient warmth, Chester instinctively judged, made necessary a reappraisal of Miss Robinson. Who was she this evening?

The round man's gaze wandered again over Victoria, Lucian and Charles; his gaze fondled their new accessories and mannerisms. There, with Mr. Wise, was The Grand

Impresario. Arguing contracts. Smiling grandly, his blue eyes so frankly knowing. And Mr. Cohen . . . Mr. Cohen? That brought an outright smile to Chester's lips. Yet, a moment later, he wondered with chagrin whether the liberty he had just taken with Mr. Wise was a result of Mr. Wise or of the game. Of Mr. Wise, he persisted in thinking, remarking again his slouch, his rude nose, his black and shifty eyes.

But he knew better. And it appeared to him then that the game could be a trap even for him. For how do you address an actor playing a role defined only by himself? And, if you dislike another—another, for example, as cunning as Mr. Wise—how are you to know whether your dislike is registered by him as applause? He would have to define the roles of the others; he would, for his own satisfaction, want to know why each had chosen his role; and, because it would be embarrassing to be himself on a stage of actors, he would do best to—he had thought he would only look in on the game—find robes for himself that would allow him to be Chester and, he thought with a smile, a bit less.

Wonderfully, Chester had lost the thread of Simon's conversation. For the cave-chested English Instructor was saying, "I number everything. I record the numbers in a ledger which I keep hidden among my shirts."

"I'm very glad you do that. Prudence, my dear boy, is a great virtue," Chester said and then gave his undivided attention to Simon, posing questions in the manner of a somewhat absent-minded older man. Simon described a fear he had—that he would be attacked and robbed again. "After all," he said, "why not? If they came once and escaped with everything they could carry—though how badly they selected their 'loot'—why should they not come a second time?" His tone, Chester thought, was more melodramatic than Simonatic. As if Simon enjoyed talking of this.

"I have begun a paper on Dostoevsky," Edgar had said, touching Max at the elbow, leading him to stand behind the chaise longue, "and I would appreciate your assistance, your advice."

Max had not seemed particularly pleased at the idea of Edgar's project. But Edgar had kept him at his side by the force of his smile and rhetoric.

"His villains. Think of the wealth of the Russian's villains, of how admirable they are for their wit, their *desinvolture:* Prince Valkovsky, Prince Stavrogin, and Svidrigailov. Briefly, to his more interesting villains, to his—shall I say?—more villainous villains, he attaches titles, money and power. To the others, those with 'hope,' he gives but ideas. And ideas—would you not say?—make one peevish.

"Svidrigailov has no need of ideas, of explanations, excuses and rationalizations. He is. He is evil. He is—need I mention?—my favorite. But his suicide can only be accepted with a grain of salt, salt with a particularly sugary taste. Didn't the Russian hold something back from us? Didn't Svidrigailov, rather than commit suicide (over the image of a child!), go on to, let us say, Germany, where he changed his name and started an automobile factory? Isn't the Russian, 'ultimately,' a mean little sentimentalist who creates proper demons only to punish them? Who unmasks 'nice' girls only from the needs of a desperate—see, Max, I too have come to appreciate the psychological approach—inferiority complex?

"No. I make too many generalities. I anticipate the results of years of study. But, coming back to the advice I would like of you, don't you think it would be as good a

jumping-off place as any to tackle Dostoevsky from the aspect of his two kinds of villains? the noble Svidrigailovs
and the unhappy Ivans?"

Max said that that was a good place to begin a study.

"You are changed, Max. A headache, perhaps? I really
expected more than this. You can't give me hints? I mean,
after all, I intend to deal with a subject with which you, of
all my acquaintances, are the most familiar. No. I know
what you are thinking. That the Ivans, the Raskolnikovs,
are all students, embedded in their miserable rooms, poor,
proud, with, as it were, no exit. Yes, I agree. That deserves
some development. The yellow water the Russian likes to
describe, the fog, the night, the miserable neighborhood he
invariably chooses for his setting. But doesn't that seem to
you—to you, Max—perverse? Simply, perverse. Encouraging his vice. No, let us recognize perversity as perversity,
and let us value lucidity—as a friend once suggested to me
that I do. If one is lucid, one has only to open the door.
Don't you think? In short, the lucid man, the Svidrigailov,
has but a trinity of truths: pleasure, pain, and well, the
holy ghost. Pleasure being both the son and the father and
pain being the same; and the holy ghost being the very seat
of the godhead, everywhere present, looking in."

Had Donald known that his poem, *Sabbatical*, would upset Emily, he certainly would not have published it. But he
had, over the years, come to take for granted that his private life with Emily had nothing that personal that it could
not be used in a poem. As it was, in *Sabbatical*, he had
changed facts so thoroughly—it had amused and flattered
him that some should have seen aspects of various of the
Wolgamuts in the poem's subject—the teacher—that it
would be no less than far-fetched to say that the subject

was anything other than general. And, he reasoned to himself, if his poem had upset Emily, that upset could well be called therapy. Seeing that one's *malaise* was generalizable, was infinitely more than particular, should indeed ultimately benefit one. Probably, her present nervosity had more to do with change of life, with that sad realization of youth forever finished, and consequently so much more sad that she should now assume the identity of a young girl. Surely, she hurt herself as much as Jane by her awkward and unkind parody.

Were she home, he would give her a sedative. She hated that. He would offer her tea; before serving it, he would dissolve a pill in it. She always knew. But she would drink the tea and smile to herself as if she found it satisfying that he should cheat her. It made Donald feel uncomfortable; for he knew he was helping her. He had suggested to her that it might not be wise for her to come this evening; she would do better to rest at home. She had refused. She had said that he might stay home and she would go. He had said that he could not, that he was interested in seeing 'the masks.'

Donald had said to Jane: "You haven't visited us in a long time."

"No," Emily had said, laughing, "I haven't visited us in a long time."

Jane did not turn away from Emily's attack; and her gaze had to be clear, impersonal, and yet have a touch of warmth. Perhaps that's what it meant to be mature—to be able to take dislike and give pity in return. She wondered if Emily's hair, bankrupt now, had ever been rich as her own. "Do you ever walk in the Village?" Emily asked. "I found these lovely earrings there. And the people are so different, so much more free—wouldn't you say?—than the university people?"

Jane answered her calmly, mildly, wondering from time to time if anyone but her interlocutors were regarding her, if Edgar were studying her from behind a lorgnette.

Edgar approached the chaise longue.

Lucian said spiritlessly, marking Edgar's intrusion: "In the room, the Wolgamuts come and go, talking of Michelangelo."

"Think rather of Piero," Charles said, directing by example Victoria's attention to the big window.

"Pierrot?" Lucian said.

Edgar, like the others, turned to look at the big window. There, he saw reflections of people, seen very dimly, superimposed like a veil on New Jersey lights.

Victoria said: "A monk—if I remember correctly, a Cistercian—once said that the heart is horizontal and the intellect is vertical. Is that right, Carlo?"

"The intellect," Charles replied, "is neither vertical or horizontal. It is the circle, the triangle and the rectangle. It is the heptagon and the cube as well. It is all things constructed. And the heart is an organ, I believe, that has something to do with the circulation of the blood."

Victoria smiled at his answer as did Lucian and the others now standing about the chaise longue: Edgar, Chester and Simon. "Nevertheless," she said, "he was a very nice man. He said that his order had no proselytizing mission. Simply, they pray for all humanity."

"But how simply?" Edgar asked, smiling.

"He is become so serious," Victoria said. "And I was

merely thinking of Fiesole, where the monks sing so beauti-
fully."

Charles said that effects achieved through religious curi-
osity could be interesting; that the religious artist searching
to represent the invisible is forced into a true channel of
art, the search to concretize the abstract. But that was,
however, in the case of religious artists, a not untainted, a
not disinterested research. More pure to study perspective.
Or, for example, to attempt to make of many curved lines
the one straight line.

"A moment ago," Victoria said, "we were speaking of
spiritual things. And here we are again, speaking of art."

Chester said with a well-considered sententiousness:
"But which of us knows of anything more spiritual than a
straight line?"

"Dear Chester," Victoria said, "do sit here." She indicated the place Lucian occupied as if Lucian were not
there. Lucian rose and ceded his place, stretching his arms
in a more flowery than rigid cruciform.

"I would," Victoria said, letting her gaze glide from Lucian to Edgar, "like someone to pray for me. Mightn't it be
a Wolgamut effort? That one of us give up everything to
pay, by his sacrifice and prayers, for all our sins."

"I shall," Lucian quickly said.

"Dear Lucian."

"But only if you promise to help me to rise. To a Bishop-
ric. To a Cardinal's red."

Victoria's smile was still a bit new to her and from time
to time, she touched her lips as if to become familiar with
it. Chester and Lucian were probing each other within the
conceit of a church career for Lucian. Chester played upon
the conditions of celibacy and meditation. Lucian com-

plained of the rigidity of the Church, that it was becoming stale, that it should be wittier. He would have background music for the confessional; he would design new vestments for the clergy—less somber; he would have, as of old, jugglers and theater in the cathedral. He would promote the cult of Mary; he would honor her by amusing her. Victoria heard fragments of conversation from elsewhere. Was it Donald who brought up Luther Halverson's name?

Charles stood with Simon. The dark and lean Fine Arts Instructor listened to Simon and would have, if only by a smile, shown his amusement that Simon had invented an identity—had he not had help? could he perhaps use a suggestion?—had his own role not obliged him to be indifferent to all things.

Max stood with his back to the window, looking in on the hall, hiding there behind a cigarette. Tired. And yet, Donald thought, touch him and he will bite. What a complex of guilt! A tic with the man. "The Self-Abusive Tic." Which might be his first satiric poem. He would have to avoid the Jewish thing, though that was really integral. Intimate it. A dark little man named Midas Salacious whose touch turned wood or character to dirt, or so Midas thought.

Characterize him how? Disloyal by principle, intellectual by curse, abusive by tic. He would push politeness to its limits and when politeness collapsed, he would be a guide in hell. That the limerickal satire. For he was really, this man, an anachronism. A romantic, in fact, who had read his Dostoevsky but not his Freud. Would he, in the last line of the poem, try vainly to bite off his magical finger?

"Luther's sick," Edgar said, answering Donald who had been too discreet to ask Jane of her bearded writer. "Hepatitis. He thrives on it," he said to Max who had joined them. "Though you should see for yourself. After all, he asks about you. Jane, by the way," he said to Donald, lowering his voice as if not to embarrass Jane—but a few feet away with Emily—"is his nurse, and a more dedicated hired nurse one could not hope to find."

Victoria left Chester and Lucian.

Lucian, even as he continued his conversation with Chester, dropped onto the chaise longue where Victoria had been and reclined there somewhat as Victoria had. Chester found Victoria's absence an occasion to say to Lucian, leaning a bit towards the younger man, "Don't, dear Lucian, hope to base a career on a rather prime indelicacy for a— what should I say?—man of the cloth." Lucian laughed aloud. Less, it seemed to Chester, at the awkward way his identity and their conceit cloaked his thoughts than at his very thoughts.

Victoria wanted movement. It would be amusing, she thought, to hire cars and for them all, dressed as they were, to go for a drive through the city, stopping here and there. She approached Emily and Jane and was tapped on the shoulder from behind. Simon asked her, leaning away from Charles, "Are there any fire-escapes in the apartment?"

She replied that there was one in the maid's room and one in the sitting room.

"Do you," Simon said, "have double locks on the windows there?"

"Oh, Simon!" Victoria exclaimed. "We're twenty-seven stories up."

To Jane, she said, "What a lovely suit, my dear." And would have offered Emily a similar pleasantry but that Emily turned just then and addressed Edgar, Max and Donald.

Emily said: "I want to write a poem, a very personal poem.

"I woke up in the morning and was not here or there. Isn't that clever? I called the library to tell them not to expect me, that I was out. They said, quite all right, but do get a doctor's opinion. The doctor said, I'm very busy. Report by noon to the Park Hospital. Your carfare will be refunded.

"It's fun walking the streets unseen. You can linger where you want. Sometimes, you meet others like yourself. You bump into them. You say excuse me and you go on your way. They're probably playing hooky from the hospital. That makes you want to know what time it is. It occurs to you then that the person you just bumped into may have been playing hooky for weeks, for months and years. You wonder if you might do that. After all, you started well: you didn't take bus or subway. The doctor virtually ordered you to. You won't report to the hospital. How easy. You'll see the world. Travel free. Linger here and there. But then you wonder, if I don't help myself to get better, who will? And who knows but that the disease is degenerative, that invisibility is but a stage, and that one can fade entirely, into nothingness. You remember that, after all, you have an obligation to get well.

"In the bed next to mine in the hospital ward is a very old lady. I can tell by her voice. And I can see by the small impression her body makes beneath the bed-covers that she is tiny. Her voice comes from across a great distance. She asks, 'What are you in for?' That is strange, for I had not realized, though probably I had sensed, that I had been 'convicted' of anything. I stammer . . . She interrupts, saying, 'Never mind. It can't really be serious: this is the recovery ward.' She tells me that she entered entirely invisible and yet, look here . . . She raises her bed-covers. The poem ends on a tiny and glistening white hip bone."

10

Victoria went shopping more and more. She delighted in walking on Fifth Avenue, in her sure and thoughtful shop-to-shop manner, in her awareness of the uselessness of nearly all her purchases. Once, leaving a taxi, she noticed that she had left her umbrella on the seat, but she acted as if she had not seen it. Later, when she mentioned to one of her visitors that she had lost one of her favorite umbrellas, she smiled at herself for the half-truth. She changed clothes frequently; but that did not change her mood. She was always the same: restless and faintly amused at the things she did and could do.

People, she considered, dropped in all the time. And Lucian, were he to have his way, would be with her constantly. He thought he was her very complement. Were she to take down an art book, he would be immediately behind her, looking at it over her shoulder. If she were to look up at him in a way that clearly indicated he was interfering with her light, he would instantly find a gesture to amuse her. He wore a tweed jacket, an Ascot. He was her clown; he was sometimes, though only when they were alone together, someone more ponderous, very condescending, someone serious and stable whom Victoria would laugh at were she not so charmed by Lucian's performance. Chester too came in what might be called a costume: a brown tweed suit that gave the round man an unpressed air of good country honesty. Of course, he came less often, generally at about five, carrying his briefcase, smiling at her in the entranceway as if in expectation of slippers and a refreshing drink. Inevitably, Lucian being there, his smile turned wry, and conversation in the conjunction of Lucian and Chester was always ambiguous, so dependent on the quality of the smile that accompanied the words that Victoria paid it little attention, thinking that Chester's evident disapproval of Lucian had nothing to do with her, but only with Chester and perhaps with the rustic role he seemed to have adopted.

Once, Charles, wearing his tunic, dropped by. He offered Victoria a packet of green tea which he said was very special; he would, in fact, have to supervise its brewing. Tea was served (with little cakes Victoria had phoned for); it was admired by all—the taste was subtle; Charles was complimented. He was not displeased but nevertheless remarked that there was no doubt but that the quality of the tea could be "darker."

In general, Chester was reluctant to leave before Lucian. "Are you coming?" he asked the younger man.

"I'll stay a while, thank you."

"I know my way," Chester said.

When Chester had gone, Victoria said to Lucian—unpleasant simply because she had the opportunity to be so: "Do you have such important business with me?"

He said, "You may judge for yourself."

Victoria, at the change in his tone, smiled in that despairing manner that Lucian could not fail to take her smile as anything other than encouragement.

He said: "Young, for I was then but fifteen or sixteen years old, I found myself one day in the subway. Opposite to me was a 'gentleman' who stared at me for some time, finding in me a spectacle of one sort or another. His stare turned mocking, and I, just a boy mind you, felt all aquiver as if I were guilty of something—all young men are, are they not, guilty of one thing or another? The 'gentleman' turned to his neighbor—I assumed they were strangers and so much the worse—and whispered something into his ear. I was sure I caught the syllables: 'ho-mo.' Homosapien? What could he have had in mind? Whatever he had in mind, it struck home.

"My first year in the Fine Arts Department, I one day gave a party to which I invited some acquaintances. My tendency in those days was towards business-like suits, shoes that one has to lace. I had my hair crew-cut. I was, regardless of what I wore, undisguised. My acquaintances were, like me, young instructors, more polished surely, more social. One or two were married, to bright young button-down things who took everything for granted. The others were bachelors, traveled, witty. And I was a source of fun for them all. When I would speak, they would smile, sensing something in me that was—how shall I put it?—*manqué*. Times, I was absolutely paralyzed by my weakness. I sulked. The evening of my party, I sulked in a soft chair I had early appropriated to myself, letting my guests serve themselves. I drank a great deal and, as my mood became progressively worse, I began to glare at everyone about me, and above all at an older man who had come a guest of a guest. This gentleman had his eyes forever on me, smiling at me as if at a silly but not malicious child. Tears came to my eyes and in anger at myself, I screamed to everyone there, 'Everyone out! Everyone out!' One guest laughed in my face. The bright young wives smiled at me as if I were an entertainment. And only the older man, shaking his head understandingly, said goodnight. I remained weeping in my chair—the others acting as if I were not there, enjoying themselves. And then I ran out of the apartment, into the street after that most reasonable man. Catching him, I begged his forgiveness.

"Shall I say I became his disciple? That would be saying too much. In any event, I saw him frequently, dined with him, went to spectacles with him, and learned from him to be more at ease, to be more myself. I feel for him yet a great affection. He consoled me. And yet—I wonder if you will believe me, Victoria—never in the way he might have liked."

He regarded Victoria candidly.

Victoria said, smiling faintly, "Why shouldn't I believe you?"

At lunch in the sitting room one day, Chester told Victoria that he did not approve of The Game. He was, however, entertaining enough, making it clear when he said, "One should not play with one's identity," that he was presently and heavy-handedly playing just that way. He said: "I have never regarded myself as a moral person. I pay with interest for my sins by the inconveniences they bring in their train. In short, I am moral only in so far as I would like to control not the action but its consequences. Yet, I do object at having an action of mine embroil another. Also, I object when someone envisages actions for which he will pay less than another, a perhaps innocent other."

"What exactly do you have in mind?"

"Generalities," he replied, smiling candidly. "And well, one specific."

"Which is?"

"Lucian."

"Lucian?"

"I do not think the young man is fully trustworthy."

"Dear Chester, what do you think I will trust him with?"

Her reply, she considered a bit later, had not been kind. But Chester had been up to it. He had changed the subject of their conversation gracefully, talked with ease of the charms of country-living, of the charms of her house in Connecticut. He had indicated that he would like to visit there again, for the natural, the relaxed atmosphere.

She would, as she had so often, drive alone to the country. But she gave in to an impulse to phone Max at the university. And once connected with the switchboard there, she asked for Lucian. Easier to be with him than any other. He put her, yes, on a pedestal, but only to dedicate clever verse to her. And how quick he was to meet her mood. If she would, it happened but rarely, turn somber, he might assume the condescending manner—as if he had had a difficult past which he had overcome—that way allowing her to be amused by him, or, to take him quite seriously, regard him as more a fool than a clown, and even blame him for her mood. She felt that all she had to do was snap her fingers and she would have another Lucian.

They drove to Connecticut. He sat back on his side of the seat, making pleasant, condescending conversation. Once at her home, he acted the gentleman farmer, more English than New Englandish. She did not believe a word of his confession. She did not think that there was a base or essence in Lucian; he was composed of air. His English country gentleman delighted her. He missed a stick; he found a pipe in his breast pocket. And, stocky in his tweed jacket, he seemed pink for the late autumn weather and not because pink was, as she had thought, his color. They toured her property, a pleasant walk, she leaning on his arm.

One Saturday afternoon, Chester, Charles and Lucian dropped in. The successive arrivals made for not the slightest commotion; it was as if each of the three took her hall for his sitting room and the others present for members— more or less liked—of the household. It was somewhat grey outside, a smoky sort of day in New Jersey, with the sun not far, but never quite in sight. The hall was warm enough; Victoria offered drinks. Chester suggested they listen to the radio broadcast of an opera; he had, he said, a weakness for Italian opera. Charles, seated not far from and with his back to the window—to take the best advantage of the light—looked up from his book to smile slightly at that. Lucian and Victoria played, on Lucian's suggestion, gin rummy. Chester brought a chair to the table and sat down at Victoria's side. He watched the game and occasionally commented on the quality of voice of the opera singers. Lucian recounted *gaffes* he had witnessed at the opera.

Victoria did not think they had been playing cards for even an hour, but it was already nearly dark outside; days were so short. Time went so quickly in the presence of her friends, but she was, just the same, restless. In her bedroom, she phoned Max at his residence hotel. He said he would be busy later; he would come now, if she liked. She said he need not bother.

Returning to the card table, she said that Mr. Wise had just called.

"Is he well?" asked Lucian.

"He is busy," Victoria replied.

Chester sang Max's praise. He said that Mr. Wise was, except for Donald Marwel—who, being "creative" could hardly be classed with the other—the most industrious of the Wolgamuts. He was, Chester informed them, publishing here and there; shortly, he would surely be invited by a book club to help them choose what people should read. Industry, he moralized, is sagacious; and ambition, he added, is witty. Lucian was not to be outdone in pleasing Victoria. He spoke of the difficulties Max had probably experienced in escaping his *milieu*, of the credit due him for his dedication to scholarship.

The opera was in its last agonies when Max, in spite of the little encouragement Victoria had given him, arrived. He wore no tie and had not shaven that day. His manner—he was surely deceived to see the others—was one of caution, as if, Victoria considered, he had prepared to do battle with her, to be wearily and scratchingly unshaven, but now had to change tactics to deal with the three others. They regarded him with a certain amiability. And Max, cautious or not, had a quality of being off-balance that added a nice tension to a room.

"I've heard," Victoria said, "that you are now in vogue.

Do you so value your successes that you will not tell me of them?"

"He's probably," Lucian said, looking up from his cards to smile at Max, "too busy to do so."

Max said that he had never considered that Victoria could be interested in the kind of articles he wrote. Lucian said that he, for one, quite agreed that articles of scholarship could interest only the author, and, other than textually, the author's departmental chairman.

The opera had just finished. Chester had sighed with the sobbing tenor who, as a final gesture, had cried out feelingfully over the soprano's body, "*Morta!*" He stood by the radio, his hand on the switch, allowing himself the pleasure of listening a moment to the chorus of bravos and the roar of applause that was greeting the revived singers. "Do you like opera, Mr. Wise?" he asked when he had silenced the radio and taken a seat. "I have a weakness for Italian opera . . ." He talked on, like an old man who must apologize for his preferences.

In short, they gently mocked Max in everything they said, and they went from Verdi to Piero. Max smiled in that way of his; Lucian flashed Victoria an imitation of that smile. Max stood slouched and ironic; perhaps he was suffering from one of his famous headaches. In any event, he soon said that he had to be going.

Victoria said that she would accompany him out. It was such in the hall that her statement occasioned not a smile.

She asked him where he was going.

He replied that he was going downtown, to sit up with a sick friend.

"May I drive you there?"

"You needn't bother."

She smiled and insisted.

In Peregrine Moth, driving downtown, he was no less distant if no less himself. Now and then, he rubbed the back of his neck. Victoria suggested that the cause of his headaches might be his eyes and perhaps he should wear glasses. He said that he did when he worked. She spoke of a play she had seen the evening before.

Max told her where to leave the Drive, and then indicated to her a corner where she could let him off.

She maneuvered, however, into a rather dark place just by the river.

*   *   *

Victoria called several people to tell them she was indisposed. The pains seemed stronger. Crouched on her bed, hugging her knees to her chin, she fought not to take another pill. The doctor, of course, would say yes, she might. One extra every three hours.

The morning of the fourth day, she felt well enough—though still weak and a bit dull—to think of going out. She did not bother to make up her face or give much attention to the clothes she wore; she was too tired to sit long before her mirror. She did, however, give a stroke or two to her hair; and she remarked that if she had suffered less this time, it was not evident in her skin or features. She was very pale and there were, about the corners of her eyes, networks of just perceptible lines. She would, simply, avoid the campus.

Only in the street did she realize that she had forgotten her umbrella, and then, with a smile, that she had forgotten as well her purse with her money and keys. Never mind. Her maid was there to open the door. It was a grey day; mist hung thinly over the river. She walked in the park that ran towards the river to the Drive. She felt a bit like an invalid and little things gave her pleasure: the trees which were so scrawny; a mittened and ear-muffed child playing under the maternal eye of his mother or nurse. Leaves were shriveled and crisp on the ground. For minutes at a time, she was quite without a thought. From time to time, she rested on a bench, clasping the collar of her coat to her neck. And for no reason at all, her lips were then trembling and she was crying.

11

Edgar was often in Luther Halverson's apartment. He
might drop in any time and stay twenty minutes or several
hours. Luther was always home; Jane Robinson was there
most of the time. She was considerably changed: she
seemed a bit older, and she could, when she wanted to, be
very capable. Not long before, Edgar had thought that
with a little encouragement, she could have become his bed-
mate. She had admired him; perhaps she still did, but now,
Edgar sensed, she wanted him to recognize in her "someone
on the other side of the fence," an opponent certain of her
convictions, or nearly so. He sensed as well that he was
valued by Jane as a witness. Curious person. She had under-
taken to nurse Luther; she paid his rent, his doctor bills; she
purchased his food and, having given up on breaking him

of his habit, paid for that as well. From time to time, she
tried to put order in his apartment; she bought bed linen;
the typewriter was moved out of the way to a corner of
the room; she installed a floor lamp behind the soft chair
where she often did her studying. Once Edgar arrived
when she was in the midst of cleaning; she was virtually
unrecognizable wearing a towel turbaned about her head, a
grey, formless smock. She cooked for her patient and herself: fish, lean steaks, vegetables in season. It was an unre-
warding mission. Luther's condition did not improve. He
had lost weight; Jane mentioned one day that he was losing
his hair, but that was not yet evident to Edgar. His eyes,
towards evening, might become feverishly bright.

Luther said that there was nothing left.

"I don't understand," Jane said, looking up from her
study.

"I believe he wants to say," Edgar explained, "that he
does not exist."

She almost smiled. But she said to Luther, "Can't you
admit that you need help?"

Useless to address a question to Luther. The rare words
he uttered seemed as accidental as they were elliptical; and
if, some weeks before, he might have smiled when spoken
to, he now seemed not to hear at all.

Between Max and Jane there was an uncomfortable
truce. She did her best to ignore the Russian scholar; she
would have liked to mock him. And he, though he probably understood as well as anyone Jane's motives for nurs-
ing Luther, treated her with deference. When he had first
come, he had been surprised to see Luther so unwell. He
had offered Jane money to help care for him; she had re-

fused, saying she could manage that by herself. Did he feel that he could do no better than Jane? In any event, here he rarely smiled; he was rarely clever; often, he would sit on a straight chair, all hung over himself.

At night, street lights filled the room with moving shadows; smoke drifted, rich, sweet. Max might be sitting in his hangdog way; Jane might be studying, the beam of her lamp covering the book in her lap; Luther might be lying across his bed; and Edgar would be watching, perhaps playing with his stick. Luther might sit up. A peculiar picture. He seemed to be, though perfectly immobile, reaching out, trying to embrace a thousand ideas to form them into one truth. He might mutter something. Edgar would cock his ear and say, "What's that? What's that, my friend?" But Luther's moments of truth were rare and not durable. These seances ended with the sick man coming to with just the force to roll a cigarette. And then Jane, indifferently, and to Edgar's amusement, might refer to Luther as Buddha.

She studied geology, taking notes.

Edgar said that he admired Luther. He said that no doubt Luther, through efforts of will, meant to conquer his body and his despair. And he said that he was waiting for the moment when Luther would radiate light.

Max was not present; Luther was in bed; and Jane was seated in the soft chair. Though she had a book open in her lap, she did not give the impression that she had now, or could have had just before, the patience to read. Occasionally, she brushed her hair back from her eyes; occasionally, she looked at Edgar who had sat down at the foot of Lu-

ther's bed. Edgar asked Luther how he was; he did not expect an answer. Luther's head was in shadows, too low beneath the window to be more than touched by street light.
Seen from this perspective, his face was elongated; his eyes
were open.

At first, Jane whispered as does a nurse in the presence of
a sleeping patient. But then, as if gaining courage, she raised
her voice a bit. She spoke of people who were "unredeemable." She said: "The chairman of the board has a big rub-
ber stamp and he inks it on his pad and stamps across a file
'unredeemable.' Then we put the person away, lock him up
out of our sight. And forget him. Isn't that terrible? Cures
are possible, they say. With time. With a great deal of time.
And, with scientific progress. But just the same, cures are
rare. Like generally, if you say good-bye, it's really good-
bye. Isn't that as it should be? Buddha says yes and he's
speaking of his wife. Oh, Buddha's a brave man. He'll lock
a person up because it's right to do that and who but
Buddha should know what's right? Isn't he right? I mean,
Edgar, aren't there people who are unredeemable? Who
add nothing to society? A blind man can weave a basket. A
deaf man can write symphonies. But the unredeemable—
they're just a burden.

"Buddha phoned me this afternoon. There are more
Buddhas than you know of, Edgar. There are Buddhas and
unredeemables. He asked me to sit with his wife while he
went out. 'Be very gentle,' he said. 'She's disturbed.'

"She seemed so small on her sofa. All the books in the
room. And the nice reproductions on the walls. And a vase
of flowers by the phone. Everything so neat and nice. She
said hello, but I wonder if she knew who I was. She held a
magazine. But that was just to keep her hands occupied, for

she'd leaf through it, slowly, and then again. And then poof, she was gone. She'd have the blankest look, the waxiest look. Her eyes never even blinked. Knock, knock, who's there? No one. No one at all. I was almost sick. My hands were all wet and cold. But then I realized something—Buddha's first lesson—: I was happy it wasn't me. Why shouldn't I have been happy? Maybe that's the part of the burden you can't get rid of—that you have to live with the idea that you're happy it's not you.

"That's not the funniest. Like the oldest of women who wakes from a nap and finds that a visitor is still there, she came to and recognized me. She smiled so nicely and said, 'You know, Jane, every time we play Monopoly, I think it's raining outside.' "

During Jane's speech, Edgar had occasionally smiled at her, occasionally looked at Luther. Once, Edgar had seen him wet his lips. That was the most emotion the speech had aroused in him.

After that day, there were times when Jane set to work cleaning the apartment in such a hurried and thorough way that Edgar had the impression she was getting ready to close the apartment, pack her bags and catch a train.

One evening, Max looked up and said: "What if there's a lucidity beyond that of seeing everything against a background of pain and suffering? Why not? Why should we think—no—why should I think that I've seen it all? That I know all there is to know? I think I see clearly, but perhaps I see only my chains. Do you know how chained I am? Ask me, 'Mr. Wise, who are you?' I'll answer that I'm an Assistant Professor of Russian Literature, that I hope that one

day I'll be a full professor. That's one answer. There are
others. I'm a Jew. Born a Jew, chained by being a Jew. I'm
a stranger in your world, on its periphery. Can I ever be at
home with Gentiles? Excuse me, with Christians. I'm a
New Yorker, a Bronx-boy. That means I have roots only
in the city, in neighborhoods, and the lower the better. I'm
like a fly, knowing the swatter's close by, but not where,
and tired of buzzing in circles. Everybody tells me I'm a
fly. Everybody knows who I am and that's like mockery.
But what if I'm not any one of those things? What if identity is the first false step? What if, asked who I am, I were
to reply, believing it, 'I am.' Simply, 'I am.'

"Now look at me. When I walk down the street, I don't
bow to my chairman or smile only at my peers. I smile at
everyone and everything. I'm not pursuing a career which
brings me rewards one day each month, but I'm reaping
rewards every second of the minute, every minute of the
day. In being. I compete with no one; I have no enemies.
Think of the burdens removed. You'll say that my happiness will bother others, that I'll make new enemies in spite
of myself. No importance. A man hits me; I'll thank him he
does no worse. A denial of personality becomes a denial of
violence." He was smiling at himself as if at a fool; and
Edgar smiled at him in an immensely polite way.

But Max did not give up on thoughts of this sort.
"Maybe it's all a question of will. Have you ever fasted?
Once, I said to myself that I'd beat the headache. I went
walking. A clear, cold night. And I concentrated every
force I have on seeing the inside of my head, on seeing the
blood vessels there, and the pressure, and the very cells that
were pushing in. I saw it all. For a second. But I saw the

whole business and that very instant, the headache was gone.

"What does everyone want? Happiness. Isn't that so? So why do they go looking for a million other things? For money? For position? It's stupid. All you have to do is be. What have I now that's so precious that I wouldn't give it up for happiness, for harmony? For twenty-four hours a day of happiness? Will. By the exercise of will to become without will. To find myself purified. To be able to walk, head up, and look at the sky. Not for thirty seconds and two minutes, but to timelessly study the sky, or the earth, or the river and the sea. Can you imagine that? Just to stand and watch? To smile because you're in harmony, in unity with the sea and sky.

"What if death's a lie? Or, if it isn't a lie, what if we were to lie that it's a lie? Allow the lie. There is no death. Think of David before the Ark of the Covenant. Eighty years old and he danced with all the joy of a child. Think of that. Of music for the pleasure of music. Violinists floating in the sky. A woman said to David, 'Look here, old man, you're making a fool of yourself.' Why David couldn't care less. He was free. He knew there was no death. Then, all the doors open. You're capable of performing miracles, of willing them. You're the example for the world and you can change the world. And think, as long as you accept death as inevitable, as a truth, you're miserable, you're afraid. You don't see beyond the one fact. What values can you have when you're mocked by death? Transient values. Why hold on to them? We live in misery if we live clearly. But go beyond. Go beyond that.

"Deny death. Finish it off. Administer the *coup de grâce*. And then, like a burst of light, you're free. Listen, there are moments when everything is in place, when suddenly you realize that the pain is gone. And your mind is clear of everything but well-being and gratitude."

Jane paid little attention to Max's speech. Luther might be sitting up, smiling; his expression might be blank, he flat on his back, his eyes open. In any event, he gave no sign that he heard anything. Edgar encouraged Max. And Max, whose smile as he spoke was never quite free of a twist of irony, did not, mocking himself, mind the mockery of Edgar.

"Outside of time, one is in the fifth dimension."

"Do you know Soutine? You smile at my choice? He paints the living and they are dead. He paints the dead and they are alive. Didn't Christ say something like that? For Soutine, a slab of meat has more life than a living person. It drips life. Things become one."

"All right, I throw over my identity. I'm no longer Max. I give up my studies, my ambitions, and I walk through the gates. I'm walking on clouds. Here. That's the beauty of it. Walking on clouds here on earth. I don't see things as before. A cough at night, what's that to me? I have the way. I can show you the way if you want to be shown. Give up everything and you will have everything. Right? Pity is nothing anyhow, and what else have I ever offered? If one becomes tired of being useless . . . walk through the gates."

"My friends, I am troubled. Last night, I dreamed of my parents. They died, you know, of cancers. A most miserable disease. A disease I, Chaim Soutine, would have to say is a disease of life. Virulent life. Attacked by life. Thus, they entered, on the wings of pain, into that fifth dimension. But I dreamed last night not of that entry, but of the months before, of the suffering before. My friends, that suffering was beyond conception. But what matter that suffering if they did arrive? There's the answer. What matter the suffering of little children if they do arrive? No matter. Suffering for them is relative. They suffer in ten years what we suffer in thirty, in fifty. Right?

"Well, there's the problem: whether the end justifies the means. For finally, to achieve the fifth dimension, I must surrender everything. Even my pleasure at the suffering of others. But, I'd like to bargain. I'd like to do it all on the installment plan. I'll give up the suffering of the blacks for a bit of the fifth dimension. And then tomorrow, I'll give up the yellow race for a bit more."

Edgar was laughing.

"And not only bargain. I want to taste the goods. I want not only to see that fifth dimension here on earth—that's easy, we've examples of people who've seen it everyday and everywhere—but to have a bite of the eternal before I sacrifice blacks, yellows, and above all, my treasure-house, the Jews. Like I mean, Chaim might be right, but Chaim might be wrong. What if the life of a cell is for us death? What if the life of the tiny merging organisms is death? No. Surely, life continues in one way or another. Matter, we are taught, remains matter. But what if matter is less matter than I now have?"

12

Edgar had, for a week now—since Jane Robinson had stopped appearing at Luther Halverson's apartment—assumed in his way the charge of Luther, providing him with occasional company, occasionally with foodstuffs, occasionally with marijuana.

Once, when Edgar arrived at the apartment, Luther was out. The sick man could have taken off; he could have, in a fit of depression, done worse. It amused Edgar to think that he had gone out to satisfy his habit. He returned. He gave no sign that he was high; he was only himself. He was a sight; his street clothes were too large for him; he wore a faded red shirt. This man had never been a runner. His beard untrimmed, he looked like one of those Village poets who at four in the morning, when the bars have closed, wander the streets slowly, tall and unseeing.

Edgar helped him into bed. He warned him that in his condition, he had no right to go out; that were he to faint in the street, he would be swept up, as it were, and deposited in a city hospital ward. He sat by him and said that if there was an answer to his own fears, Luther alone had the key. He described his nightmares. The faces of children that became monstrous. A chase through narrow city streets—which he elaborated and dramatized in many little ways. He sensed that Luther heard every word he said and that he did not speak because he was just too weak, too weary.

Edgar invited the Wolgamuts to play The Game at Luther's apartment.

No expense was too great for him to make for his friends. He provided cushions to use as seats; a long table to present a snack; an oriental cloth to cover the table and heavy candelabra for the lighting of it. He had the place cleaned from top to bottom; that hardly helped; he bought straw mats for the floor. He went to buy sandwiches and ordered instead six chickens; he specified they were to be roasted over embers, basted to be crisp and golden; he ordered a roast beef of enormous proportions. Tall bottles of Rhine wine, Bordeaux. It was like Christmas: delivery-men arriving all through the afternoon, Edgar setting to work unwrapping packages, finding a place for this and that. Luther sat up part of the day and towards evening developed a fever. Edgar put him to bed, and then, having covered him, returned to the bed and adjusted the covers this way and that. The room was lit only by the light which came from the street and by the candles in the pair of candelabra. Luther was nearly hidden in shadows.

Simon Parr was the first to arrive. The cave-chested English Instructor entered limping, using a cane. His arm was in a sling. He nodded to Edgar who was smiling in his very polite way and took the one soft chair—the right of a man as maimed as himself. His costume delighted Edgar as did his regard which was new and supercilious. Yet, as they made small conversation, waiting for the others, as Simon's eyes grew accustomed to the dim light, Edgar remarked in his confrère a growing wariness. Simon searched the walls for books, for phonograph records; he found but the face of Luther and with an abrupt gesture, nearly jerking his arm from his sling (credit to him for he winced even as he spoke), he demanded: "Who is that?"

"You remember Luther," Edgar said.

Simon smiled. Luther was surely here in a role, under Edgar's direction.

Victoria arrived with Lucian Whittier, Chester Mawr and Charles Rizzo. Charles, elegant in black tunic, black gloves, was at Victoria's right; Lucian, in dinner clothes, was at her left. Chester too was in dinner clothes, but too discreet to make a fourth in their line, he stood a bit behind them, round and urbane. Victoria wore a white gown, a short black caracul coat, lustrous in the light; her hair was swept up; she wore gold pendant earrings. She seemed about thirty-five, the kind of woman who could never make an ungraceful move.

Lucian exclaimed: "When have I last been in such a charming place! What an extravagant imagination. And

look, kind Edgar has provided us with a beggar man . . ."
he indicated Simon who nodded a greeting ". . . and a
dead man. Is it a wake, Edgar? Shall we stay, Vickie?"

"I have never been to a wake," Victoria said.

"It is," Edgar said, "less frivolous than a wake."

"How enigmatic," Victoria said and arranged herself on
a cushion.

Lucian sat beside her. Charles knelt a bit behind them,
making of them a triangular composition—a bit off-balance
and more interesting for that—in black and white relieved
by and sparkling in the gold of Victoria's earrings.

Chester found a place facing them.

"Candlelight suits you," he said to Victoria.

He turned to Edgar as if for confirmation and was less
impressed by the display on the table. He disliked food that
was so clearly food, and the proximity of several basted
chickens was not to his taste; nor was the vivid, congealing,
roast beef red.

Edgar asked if he might serve a bit of wine.

Lucian mused: "The air of a wake. A beggar man and a
dead man."

"The 'beggar,'" Simon informed them, "is not of Edgar's invention."

"My dear boy," Chester said, "what ever did happen to
you?"

Charles whispered to Victoria.

Victoria said, "Charles thinks Simon has had another call
from Western Union. Whatever that means."

Edgar greeted Jane Robinson and the poet, Donald Marwel, at the door. Jane wore a suit, a sober thing; her hair
was not unattractively arranged in a knot; she wore heels

and carried a small and neat bag. Donald seemed to have lost a bit of weight; there was the faintest indication of hollows under his eyes.

Edgar said, "How glad I am you could both come. Emily isn't ill, is she?"

Jane smiled calmly in the face of his malice. She searched out, in shadows, the form of Luther. And even as Donald answered Edgar, saying that Emily was visiting family in New England, he too looked at the inanimate form in the bed.

"Will she be away long?"

"Perhaps," Donald answered, smiling mildly.

Max arrived a bit disheveled. He made a general and extravagant bow to the company, taking in everything, it seemed, in a glance: Luther and Edgar, Jane and Donald, Chester across from Victoria, Lucian and Charles. Then, smiling in his way, he took a place in shadows, at a distance from the others.

Simon said: "I returned home from the university and you can imagine my surprise when, having locked and double-locked the door of my apartment after me, I found, seated in my living room, five enormous Negroes. They wore uniforms somewhat like those worn by paratroops; they had heavy 'jumpshoes' and were very neat. Clearly, they had been waiting for my arrival, and interestingly enough, they had disturbed absolutely nothing. As I stood there, they formed, as in a rite, a circle about me. One of them—you can see how big they were—picked me up off the floor by my necktie and held me like that for a moment as if to permit me to fully appreciate the helplessness of my situation; and then he slapped me across the face, a most stunning blow, releasing me at the same time. I collapsed to all fours; I remember that I saw only their shoes. There was at this time a pause that was not repeated in their 'activities.' Perhaps to allow me to defend myself orally or physically. I saw no reason to waste words on these brutes; they could not understand anything I might say. And as for the physical, surely any resistance on my part would have brought about a worse ordeal than the one I did experience. But let me mention now that all during this time of pause, as before and after, the brutes never said a word, and their expressions—if such can be called the immobility of their expressionless and thick-featured faces—never changed. A second 'paratroop' picked me up exactly as had the first and hit me scientifically, I would say, in the solar plexus. I was absolutely deprived of breath and that lasted for an intolerable time during which the 'rite,' for I will call it that, continued. The third bent to me and taking hold of my arm, broke it at the elbow with but a twist of his wrist. The fourth did the same with my ankle. The fifth turned me onto my back and leaning over me, raised his fist—I can see it now and I only hope that none of you will ever experience the terror of such a sight—raised his fist as if it were a hammer and he was about to smash my head in. I then lost consciousness and assume that the fist never hit me, that it had been meant as a threat, a melodramatic forget-me-not.

"When I came to, I of course phoned the police. I was told that they had heard of these 'paratroops.' They are a Harlem gang who break into apartments, but who do not steal. Their methods of entry can, as required, be ingenious, daring, or both, and there is, it seems, no protection against them. If there is no willing domestic to allow them in, they will use a fire escape. If there is no convenient fire escape, they lower ropes from the roof to your window; if there are bars on your window, they saw through them. They are known to have entered an otherwise impregnable apartment through the floor of the apartment above.

"The police gave me photographs of suspects, but needless to say, any one of those photographed brutes could have been part of the gang."

Simon's story aroused among the Wolgamuts many smiles, some laughter.

"It's not fair," Lucian, a bit later, protested to Edgar.

"Yes?"

"Yes?" Lucian allowed himself, mocking his host. "Yes, it's not at all fair. How are we to guess what you have there . . ." nodding towards Luther " . . . represented when the subject is dead?"

"You are cold."

"Am I?"

"Then," he said, "you will answer questions for him?"

"One from each of you."

"A new game?" Donald asked.

It was explained to Donald, Jane and Max that there was a meaning to Luther's pose.

For Jane, seeing Luther was the best of therapies. Even as Donald had suggested when Edgar had invited them to this evening, it was important for her to face her decision now to better live with it later. Luther had given up on life; he was the butt of jokes. There was nothing she could do for him and no one could ever reproach her for not having done her best. Period. It required an effort of will to be a man; it required a self-understanding and a willing submission. Sometime, in one's life, one had to say: I need help. And in all humility put oneself into the hands of another.

Had she been drawn to him by his weaknesses? By his need of speed, his distrust of words, of people? She had been in love with herself. Narcissistic. And her betrayals of Luther had been but self-punishment—her first signs of health. How clear, if one remained dispassionate, things could become.

She stood with Donald waiting behind some others, a step or two from the table. She was grateful for Donald, for his patience and kindness, for the fine understanding that existed between them. She had wanted to speak to him of Luther; he had said that it was not necessary, as if afraid that such a conversation could only hurt and embarrass her. He was too gentle. She knew that her relationship with Luther was like a wound, but the telling of it would have been for her the story of the beginning of her cure. He thought of the others generously; she thought them foolish. Perhaps age would mellow her too. She doubted it. She thought them wrong. He had such a funny shape, such a heavy rear. He was twice her age; he was a professor and she was a student. She cared nothing for conventions.

Charles' difficulty—again in his pose behind Victoria and Lucian—was his gloves. He would have to remove them to attack the chicken. He put his plate down. His gloves were fine and skin-tight and consequently he had to proceed very slowly. He pulled a glove at the little finger perhaps a millimeter, and then, one by one, at the other fingers. The process was repeated five or six times; he worked with infinite patience. Some of the Wolgamuts regarded him, smiling in their ways. Charles went on to the second glove and removed that with equal grace.

Not one of the chickens remained whole. And the roast

beef, somewhat reduced, nevertheless presented the same large face. Edgar, having served Simon and having vainly asked Luther if he would join the others in a bite, now was going about the room replenishing wine glasses.

Victoria asked Edgar: "Do we have the right to examine your tableau more closely?"

"By all means," Edgar replied. "Will you want light?"

He brought a candelabrum from the table and placed it on the windowsill above Luther's head.

Victoria approached and studied Luther. The candles in the window were caught in a draft and the light, blowing this way and that—doubled in reflection, reflected too, now and then, in Luther's eyes—created moving planes within Luther's face. His features seemed very sharp. She saw a cold sore at the corner of his mouth, nearly hidden by his beard. She wanted to touch him, or at least to brush a bit of the soft material of her gown against him.

Lucian was at her elbow.

She turned, smiling, to him and said, "It can only be a wake."

"He does," Lucian said, "have a certain morbid pallor."

Max was smiling at Victoria from a corner of the room; he seemed to be lying on his stomach on the floor.

Jane asked Edgar in a bantering way, "Is this your idea or Max's?"

"Is that your question?" Edgar asked.

"Why do you mock him this way?"

"That question certainly deserves an answer," Edgar answered, smiling.

"Bravo, Mr. Wise," Chester said.

Max was on all fours, approaching the center of the room.

At first, it might have seemed that he was groping about for something lost; but then, by the look of contentment that covered his face—as if he were really pleased with himself—it became clear that it was his intention to crawl through the Wolgamuts' midst, to entertain them perhaps.

"Now what does that represent?" Lucian asked.

"It seems to fancy itself a dog," Charles said.

"It's a horse," Lucian said, "searching for a rider."

Max raised his head, smiling an invitation at Lucian.

"Go ahead," Chester urged the younger man.

"No sport," Lucian said, "without spurs."

Jane said to Donald: "Don't you think it's particularly Russian of him to hold it against us that he thinks himself a dog, a beast, a rat?"

Max whimpered as if hurt to the quick.

Lucian said, "Why not put him on a leash and give him a bone?"

Max snarled.

Lucian backed away in mock fright and picking up a chicken bone at random from a plate, waved it tantalizingly before Max.

Victoria said, "All he wants is some affection."

She bent to pet the back of his neck.

Max threw his head around and snapped at her fingers.

"Enough of that!" Lucian exclaimed, putting himself between Max and Victoria. He threatened Max with his foot; Max retreated, crawling backwards. Lucian cracked a whip and Max backed into a corner.

Chester asked Edgar: "If your friend is not dead, is he meditating?"

"Warm," Edgar answered.

"I know," Victoria said. "He's praying."

"Ah?"

"He's praying for all of us."

"And why should he not be?" Edgar said heartily.

"But what can we do for him?" Victoria asked. "We owe him so much."

"Why not leave him alone?" Jane said.

Victoria answered Jane's smile warmly and said, as if not having heard her, "We should honor him."

"Marwel will write a poem," Charles said.

Donald smiled good-naturedly.

"We should pray with him," Lucian said and dropped to his knees.

Victoria knelt on a cushion. Even Simon knelt, though with difficulty. Only Jane and Edgar remained standing, one smiling mockingly, the other very politely. Chester and Donald remained cross-legged on cushions; Chester looked with a kind of glass eye at everything here; Donald smiled mildly, if reprovingly.

There was a moment of silence.

Then Victoria rose and going to Luther, left an earring at the side of his head.

Simon followed. He leaned his cane against the bed and walked away upright.

Max was next. Crawling to Luther, he kissed him on the cheek.

Lucian asked if the wake would now begin.

13

Edgar wondered what Luther's disappearance meant. To be sure, he might have removed himself to another neighborhood in the city, to another city in the United States, or elsewhere. Hadn't he been tempted to return to Mexico? There was, in fact, no indication as to exactly what Luther had done. His apartment had been left open; remnants of the Wolgamut evening had been everywhere. Edgar had waited an hour. And another. He had collected the more valuable and transportable of his possessions: the candelabra, the oriental cloth. Victoria's gold earring—as a memento. Leaving, thinking to hail a taxi, his possessions under his arm, his stick in his hand, he had had the idea to look in the neighborhood for Luther's car. He had seen some sports cars, though, for the most part, the cars parked in that neighborhood were dusty old things. He had passed beneath the expressway and had stood, melancholy for half a moment at the city's edge, at the river.

With Max, whom he met by chance at the Boston restaurant, he discussed the possible significations of Luther's disappearance. And seeing Max's sensitivity to the idea of Luther having done away with himself, he developed that thesis. He said that, after all, for Luther that was a way out and more. He could imagine him doing the deed. At the wheel of his car, driving at one hundred miles an hour, tempted to ram into the lights of an uncoming car. Not that. Not to go out in a blaze of glory. But to do it in silence, in a closet as it were (which would explain—would it not?—why his body and the wreckage of his car had not yet been discovered and reported). To find a deserted lake and plough into it softly, at but five miles an hour. One might, Edgar suggested, "drag" Victoria's lake to advantage.

Edgar's dreams were not pleasant, but they were not endless. He would go to bed—rarely before dawn—and would say to himself: "What shall we have tonight? Footsteps in the dark or a creaking door? Monstrous children or childish monsters?" Artifice. Dreams were pure artifice. And if he would wake in a cold sweat, cornered in a dead-end street, it would nevertheless be day and he would, entertaining himself, examine the structure of his dream, see how the effects had been achieved. In the company of his peers, he had little amusement. There was, in fact, little but the sensation of fear that interested him. Threatened, he put on a clean shirt and walked upright. In black neighborhoods, his nighttime promenade. He felt that one had no right to go on living the way he did, and yet, he longed for a disciple. He would say, "Young man, have you ever thought that paranoia is the only normal state?" The words would come easily enough. He would take his young friend's arm; they would go from bar to bar, from low neighborhood to low neighborhood, never drinking, always high. He would show him faceless faces, cock an ear to measure the violence in the air.

*   *   *

Edgar stood with Jane, Donald and Max in the hall, by the grand piano.

Chester and Simon stood between this group and the chaise longue—closer to the chaise longue—which Victoria was sharing with Lucian. Lucian was entertaining Victoria, reading her fortune in cards. Charles stood behind the chaise longue. No one was in costume: Victoria wore a pair of russet-colored sweaters, a simple skirt; Lucian wore a tweed jacket, a knitted necktie; Charles wore a correct and austere dark suit. Chester wore flannels; Simon had no bandages, sling or cane. He spoke with Chester of his summer voyage to the Greek Islands. His monologue was as organized as ever; and yet, it was not without nuances, not without wit.

Lucian turned over the queen of hearts. That was Victoria's wardrobe. A seven of clubs was a black coat with seven buttons in two uneven lines, with a high collar and a flare to the skirt. The five of hearts was a simple gown, white, trimmed sparingly with gold.

Edgar, once again, brought up the possibility of Luther having done away with himself.

Jane's smile was a bit forced. She said, "You would see it that way."

Edgar described to her, as he had to Max, the reasons that supported his thesis: the typewriter left behind, the door left open; his physical state, his mental state. Two weeks and no sign of Luther. He went on to picture for her Luther's last hour, this time embellishing his account, detailing it with knuckles gripped white about the steering wheel, faintness, fever, determination. And a final and wonderful calm as he waded, as it were, deeper and deeper into the water.

Donald smiled at Edgar's account, but said that from everything he knew of Luther, suicide was a distinct possibility. He continued in that way, no doubt in order to help Jane to learn to live with the idea of that possibility. He said that the so-called intellectual reasons for suicide were generally—from what he understood of the matter— less important than the physical state of the person. Not the hurt or the idea, but the mood and the fever.

Max had only facts to relate.

"It was two A.M. and I happened to be walking by the river. The Drive was deserted, empty. Suddenly, far off, I saw the headlights of a low-slung car, a long, black sports car. It passed me in a flash, gone in a flash. But I'd take an oath that the driver had a beard.

"In short," he said, smiling, nodding towards the big window, "Luther's out there." He said that if you wanted proof that he was alive, all you had to do was go to a turnpike, any turnpike, and wait. Only at night, to be sure. Between two and four in the morning. Have a lantern ready. And when you see a long, low, black sports car approaching at a crazy speed, wave the lantern twice. Like this. Then all you have to do is step in.

Jane said with some impatience: "With a person like Luther, everything is possible. Shouldn't I know? But there's no question in my mind that if he's not already, he will shortly be installed in some dirty place—some very dirty place—in Chicago or San Francisco. Perhaps he'll have the will to get work. Probably, he'll find someone to feed off."

Lucian was describing Victoria's entourage. His entertainment had brought Simon and Chester to the chaise longue. To honor Chester, he identified the ten of hearts as an elderly gentleman, patient to a fault, who had, of recent, turned into a nasty old nine of clubs. The jack of diamonds, however, was a young man, too modest for words, come to the capital to solve a riddle.

"Which is?" Victoria asked.

"I've forgotten," Lucian said with a smile.

"You are pompous," she said. She rose and joined the others by the piano.

Simon took her place on the chaise longue.

Conversation by the piano was polite.

*   *   *

The guests had left. Lucian, having seen the last of them to the door, returned to the hall. Victoria was reclining on the chaise longue.

"Dull?" He asked.

"Quite."

"Shall I continue your fortune?"

"Do find something else."

Lucian did. He switched off most of the lights in the hall. He arranged two lamps to provide a center of light ten or so feet in front of Victoria. Victoria, nearly hidden in shadows, smiled faintly as Lucian stepped into the center of light. He raised his hands to his face and then opened the curtains on Chester.

The round man with the cool regard said in his mellifluous way: "Dear Vickie is dull. We shall devise an entertainment for her. Call for Edgar."

The curtains opened instead, and only for an instant, on Emily.

She said sarcastically, "Is she then our queen?"

"Dear," Donald said, smiling mildly, "do try to relax."

"We could play Monopoly," Edgar said, drawing on his pipe.

"How very dull," Victoria said, reclining on her chaise longue, a tiara in her hair.

"I bring you a report from Rhodes," said cave-chested Simon, kneeling before his sovereign. "Contrary to rumors, the Colossus of Rhodes is in existence and it represents a remarkably thick-lipped individual."

"Cut off his head," Victoria dryly commented.

Two guards dragged Simon from the hall.

"The emissary of the Shah," Edgar, wearing the robes of state, announced condescendingly.

Max approached in a crouch. He wore a turban and rich robes which, however, one might have suspected were soiled within. He carried a sack over his shoulder. Before kneeling to the queen, he said in a stage whisper, smiling ironically, "It's me, the sandman."

"What have you there?" Edgar asked the oriental emissary, not bothering to face him.

"Spices and condiments, cloth for the queen's raiment."

"He lies," Lady Jane said. She stood at the window, looking forlornly beyond the castle walls. "I saw this man

when searching for Sir Galahad. He is an itinerant merchant of scorpion eggs, wasp stings and viper venom."
"Then off with his head," said the queen.

Nobles of the court, elegant in austere costumes, joined the queen to pass with her the waning hours of the day. A slow dance was performed. A magician brought a rabbit from his ear. A lute player with the gentlest and clearest of voices sang nicely for the queen.